ABORIGINAL
STORIES
OF AUSTRALIA

A. W. REED

Reed New Holland

Originally published in *Myths and Legends of Australia*
by A.W. Reed © 1965, 1971, 1976

This title published in Australia in 1999 by
Reed New Holland
an imprint of New Holland Publishers (Australia) Pty Ltd
Sydney • Auckland • London • Cape Town
14 Aquatic Drive Frenchs Forest NSW 2086 Australia
218 Lake Road Northcote Auckland New Zealand
86 Edgware Road London W2 2EA United Kingdom
80 McKenzie Street Cape Town 8001 South Africa

First published in 1980 by Reed Books Pty Ltd
Reprinted in 1982, 1984, 1988 (twice), 1990, 1991, 1993, 1994, 1997
Reprinted in 1998 and 1999 by Reed New Holland

Designer: Luisa Laino
Cover illustration: Kim Roberts
Typesetter: Midland Typesetters
Printer: Australian Print Group

National Library of Australia Cataloguing-in-Publication Data:

Reed, Alexander Wyclif, 1908–1979
Aboriginal stories of Australia

ISBN 1 87633 417 7

1. Aborigines, Australian–Legends
I. Title.

398.20994

20 19 18 17 16 15 14 13

ABORIGINAL
STORIES
OF AUSTRALIA

CONTENTS

Introduction   vii

Part I: Creation Myths
Yhi Brings Life to the World   10
The Strange Shape of Animals   13
The First Man   15
The Gift of Flowers   18
The Plague of Insects   21
The First Initiation Ceremony   25
The Wives of Baiame   32
Baiame and the Land of Women   35

Part II: Legends of Sun, Moon and Stars
Why Kookaburra Laughs at Dawn   39
The Blue Fish and the Moon   42
Wahn and the Moon God   45
Waxing and Waning Moon   49
The Husbands and Wives who Became Stars   52
Nurunderi, the two Girls, and the Evil One   55
Eagle-hawk and the Woodpeckers   64
The Seven Sisters   68
The Brush Turkeys of the Sky   74
The Dancing of Priepriggie   77

Part III: Legends of Animals
The Last of his Tribe   80
How the Animals Came to Australia   81
How Flying Fox Divided Day and Night   84

The Imprisonment of Narahdarn the Bat   89

Why Platypus Lives Alone   93

How Kangaroo Got His Tail   98

The Cat Killer   100

Glossary   105

INTRODUCTION

In recent years there has been increased interest in the Australian Aboriginals, who at one time were regarded as so primitive in their outlook and culture that little purpose was to be served by investigating and preserving their anthropological records. It is only when we are in danger of losing something that we begin to value it, and the large number of books describing the life, customs, arts, and skills of the Aboriginals is ample proof of this renewal of interest.

It is important that white Australians should appreciate the wealth of imagination displayed in Aboriginal legend. It is part of the literature of Australia. We shall not put our roots down into the soil until we have incorporated their folklore into the indigenous literature of the southern continent, and can see the land through the eyes of the primitive, clever, imaginative people who had to fight to gain their nourishment from Mother Earth. It is remarkable that in an environment of desert wastes and infertile soil, as well as in well-watered country, the imagination of the Aboriginals should produce tales that are both beautiful and amusing, and that they should find human characteristics and poetry in bird and beast, in the sky above them, in sun, moon, and stars, and even in reptiles and insects.

They lived close to the soil, these children of nature. They were dependent on her for sustenance, and in the teeming animal life and in the barren places alike they found evidence of the work of a Creator Spirit, and promise of Bullima, the after-life, where game abounded, there was soft grass to lie on, refreshing streams, and soft breezes. From their physical needs a majestic conception of nature was evolved, with beneficent spirit ancestors—and the corresponding spirits of evil that are inimical to mankind.

The legends contained in this book have been gathered from many different sources. It is a comprehensive collection which originated among different tribes and can be regarded as a typical sampling of the beliefs of Aboriginals in every part of Australia.

Coming from widely divergent sources, it is natural that there should be inconsistencies and contradictory elements. This is particularly the case in the Creation myths and the folklore concerning animals when the land was still in the Dreamtime. From some legends we learn that animals and insects were brought to life at the touch of Yhi, the Sun Goddess, and that Man, the final creation, was made in the bodily and mental form of Baiame, the Great Spirit.

Other widespread legends say that all living things first took the form of men, and gradually achieved individual characteristics as animals. This is a reasonable explanation of the origin of totemism, which exercised a considerable influence on Aboriginal life. It is a vast subject, especially as totemism took different forms in various parts of the country. The presentation of myths and legends in a form which is acceptable to the present day must necessarily depart from the spirit of the Eternal Dreamtime in many respects. To the Aboriginal the stories were not simply pleasant tales to beguile the evening hours. As Professor A.P. Elkin remarked, 'Mythology is not just a matter of words and records, but of action and life, for the cult societies, the totemic lodges, do not spend their time at meetings reciting and chanting only; they also re-enact myths, and do so because the heroes and ancestors were, in their belief, actual persons and totemic beings; what they did in the course of their labours must now be done in ritual and the places associated with them must be visited and cared for. For the most part, the details of any myth are only important because they enable the present-day men to walk the path with fidelity, which leads into the sacred dreamtime, the source of life.'*

So far as possible, continuity of theme runs through the collection, but because of the widespread origin of the tales, the reader should consider each legend as a self-contained narrative, without attempting to put it in the context of other stories in the same chapter. For this reason animals sometimes appear as men, and at other times in their natural form. Similarly

---

* *The Australian Aborigines*, A. P. Elkin, Angus & Robertson, 4th edn. 1964, p. 244.

there are several conceptions of the Father-God, the Great Spirit, Baiame. In some he is Culture hero, father and creator of his people, towards whom created man aspires; in others he is a great wirinun, plagued by faithless and foolish wives.

The value of this compilation may well lie in its representative nature. With hundreds of tribes and hundreds of languages, there was no homogeneity of nomenclature, but there was a common ethos which can be readily found by sampling the variant legends of different tribes.

An arbitrary selection of Aboriginal names for living creatures has been made and adhered to throughout in order to avoid confusion, but it will be appreciated that such names varied according to tribe and locality. A glossary of names and Aboriginal terms is given in an appendix.

Many books have been used freely as source material, but variant accounts have been compared and the tales rewritten in a form that it is hoped will appeal to readers of the present time. The modern version of Mrs Langloh Parker's books of Eulalie tradition, edited by H. Drake-Brockman and published by Angus and Robertson in 1953 are particularly valuable. *Myths and Legends of the Australian Aboriginals* by Dr W. Ramsay Smith and published by George G. Harrap & Co. in 1930 is the largest collection previously published.

A. W. Reed

Part I

Creation Myths

 Yhi Brings Life to the World

In the beginning the world lay quiet, in utter darkness. There was no vegetation, no living or moving thing on the bare bones of the mountains. No wind blew across the peaks. There was no sound to break the silence.

The world was not dead. It was asleep, waiting for the soft touch of life and light. Undead things lay asleep in icy caverns in the mountains. Somewhere in the immensity of space Yhi stirred in her sleep, waiting for the whisper of Baiame, the Great Spirit, to come to her.

Then the whisper came, the whisper that woke the world. Sleep fell away from the goddess like a garment falling to her feet. Her eyes opened and the darkness was dispelled by their shining. There were coruscations of light in her body. The endless night fled. The Nullarbor Plain was bathed in a radiance that revealed its sterile wastes.

Yhi floated down to earth and began a pilgrimage that took her far to the west, to the east, to north, and south. Where her feet rested on the ground, there the earth leaped in ecstasy. Grass, shrubs, trees, and flowers sprang from it, lifting themselves towards the radiant source of light. Yhi's tracks crossed and recrossed until the whole earth was clothed with vegetation.

Her first joyous task completed, Yhi, the sun goddess, rested on the Nullarbor Plain, looked around her, and knew that the Great Spirit was pleased with the result of her labour.

'The work of creation is well begun,' Baiame said, 'but it has only begun. The world is full of beauty, but it needs dancing life to fulfil its destiny. Take your light into the caverns of earth and see what will happen.'

Yhi rose and made her way into the gloomy spaces beneath the surface. There were no seeds there to spring to life at her touch. Harsh shadows lurked behind the light. Evil spirits shouted, 'No, no, no,' until the caverns vibrated with voices that boomed and echoed in the darkness. The shadows softened. Twinkling points of light sparkled in an opal mist. Dim forms stirred restlessly.

'Sleep, sleep, sleep,' the evil spirits wailed, but the shapes had been waiting for the caressing warmth of the sun goddess. Filmy wings opened, bodies raised themselves on long legs, metallic colours began to glow. Soon Yhi was surrounded by myriads of insects, creeping, flying, swarming from every dark corner. She retreated slowly. They followed her out into the world, into the sunshine, into the embrace of the waiting grass and leaves and flowers. The evil chanting died away and was lost in a confusion of vain echoes. There was work for the insects to do in the world, and time for play, and time to adore the goddess.

'Caves in the mountains, the eternal ice,' whispered Baiame. Yhi sped up the hill slopes, gilding their tops, shining on the snow. She disappeared into the caverns, chilled by the black ice that hung from the roofs and walls, ice that lay hard and unyielding, frozen lakes in ice-bound darkness.

Light is a hard thing, and a gentle thing. It can be fierce and relentless, it can be penetrating, it can be warm and soothing. Icicles dripped clear water. Death came to life in the water. There came a moving film over the ice. It grew deeper. Blocks of ice floated to the surface, diminished, lost their identity in the rejoicing of unimprisoned water. Vague shapes wavered and swam to the top—shapes which resolved themselves into fish, snakes, reptiles. The lake overflowed, leaped through the doorways of caves, rushed down the mountain sides, gave water to the thirsty plants, and sought the distant sea. From the river the reptiles scrambled ashore to find a new home in grass and rocks, while fish played in the leaping waters and were glad.

'There are yet more caves in the mountains,' whispered Baiame.

There was a feeling of expectancy. Yhi entered the caves again, but found no stubborn blocks of ice to test her strength. She went into cave after cave and was met by a torrent of life, of feather and fur and naked skin. Birds and animals gathered round her, singing in their own voices, racing down the slopes, choosing homes for themselves, drinking in a new world of light, colour, sound, and movement.

'It is good. My world is alive,' Baiame said.

Yhi took his hand and called in a golden voice to all the things she had brought to life.

'This is the land of Baiame. It is yours for ever, to enjoy. Baiame is the Great Spirit. He will guard you and listen to your requests. I have nearly finished my work, so you must listen to my words.

'I shall send you the seasons of summer and winter—summer with warmth which ripens fruit ready for eating, winter for sleeping while the cold winds sweep through the world and blow away the refuse of summer. These are changes that I shall send you. There are other changes that will happen to you, the creatures of my love.

'Soon I shall leave you and live far above in the sky. When you die your bodies will remain here, but your spirits will come to live with me.'

She rose from the earth and dwindled to a ball of light in the sky, and sank slowly behind the western hills. All living things sorrowed, and their hearts were filled with fear, for with the departure of Yhi darkness rushed back into the world.

Long hours passed, and sorrow was soothed by sleep. Suddenly there was a twittering of birds, for the wakeful ones had seen a glimmer of light in the east. It grew stronger and more birds joined in until there came a full-throated chorus as Yhi appeared in splendour and flooded the plains with her morning light.

One by one the birds and animals woke up, as they have done every morning since that first dawn. After the first shock of darkness they knew that day would succeed night, that there would always be a new sunrise and sunset, giving hours of daylight for work and play, and night for sleeping.

The river spirit and the lake spirit grieve most of all when Yhi sinks to rest. They long for her warmth and light. They mount up into the sky, striving with all their might to reach the sun goddess. Yhi smiles on them and they dissolve into drops of water which fall back upon the earth as rain and dew, freshening the grass and the flowers and bringing new life.

One last deed remained to be done, because the dark hours of night were frightening for some of the creatures. Yhi sent the Morning Star to herald her coming each day. Then, feeling sorry for the star in her loneliness, she gave her Bahloo, the Moon, for her husband. A sigh of satisfaction arose from the earth when the white moon sailed majestically across the sky, giving birth to myriads of stars, making a new glory in the heavens.

 ## The Strange Shape of Animals

When animals were brought to life from the frozen depths of earth by the sun goddess, who shall tell what they were like? There are some who say that they had the form of men and women, and others that they had many different shapes. We can be certain of only one thing ... that after a time they grew tired of the forms that Baiame had given them, and were seized by vague longings.

Those who lived in the water wanted to be on dry land. Those who walked on the earth wished to feel the freedom of the sky. There was not a single animal that was not possessed by this strange discontent. They grew sad and hid themselves away from Yhi. The cheerful sound of their voices was no longer heard, and the green plants wilted in sympathy with their friends the creatures.

Looking down in her slow crossing of the sky, Yhi realised that sorrow lay heavily on the earth. For the last time she descended from the sky and stood on the Nullarbor Plain. From every direction a tide of animal life flowed in towards her.

'She has come back! The goddess will listen to our requests,' they shouted.

'Come closer,' she called to them. 'Tell me what is troubling you.'

A babble of voices answered her. Waves of sound surged around her. She held up her hands.

'Stop! Stop!' she called. 'I cannot hear what you are saying when you all speak at once. One by one, please.'

She beckoned to Wombat, who craved a body that could wriggle into shady places where he could hide from others.

He was followed by Kangaroo, who wanted strong legs for leaping and a tail with which to balance himself.

Bat said he wanted wings so that he could fly through the air like a bird.

Lizard was tired of wriggling on his belly and needed legs to support himself.

Poor Platypus could not make up his mind what he wanted, and ended up with the parts of many animals.

Yhi smiled as they came and made their wants known to her. She smiled because their forms were so bizarre; she smiled tenderly because she realised that with the transfiguration of their bodies, life would change for her little creatures.

Mopoke, who has asked for large, shining eyes, would have to hide in dim places by day and hunt only at night.

Stick Insect would need to remain unmoving for hours on the branches of trees till he almost turned into a twig.

Pelican would have to learn to stand motionless with his long legs in the water before he could snap up an unwary fish.

She smiled wistfully because she knew that the granting of their wishes would not bring contentment to her little ones. The restless surge of life that seeks and demands would take them away from her. Other changes would come, suddenly or slowly, in mysterious ways, and by strange adventures. The world was to be full of change.

She dismissed them and watched them disperse to every quarter of the earth before she rose up for the last time into the sky.

The story of these changes has been told round campfires for a thousand years. When men and women came to live in the great continent, and saw the creeping, crawling, jumping, swift-running, flying, burrowing wild life on which they depended for their food, they invented strange tales to account for the habits of the creatures that Baiame had given to them. As we crouch round the embers with them, sheltered from the wind by the low fence of woven branches, let us also listen to tales that have come from the heart of a people who are closer than we are to the gods of nature.

 ## The First Man

Now the labours of Yhi, the sun goddess, were over. Her warmth and tenderness had brought living creatures to the earth and they basked in her love. Now that she had left them, they were under the care of the Great Spirit. In the spirit of Baiame was thought, intelligence, life; but it had no body.

'I cannot appear to my children and yours,' Baiame told Yhi. 'I will clothe the power of my thought in flesh. Then they will see me and know that I am indeed their Father.'

'The gods are one creation and the animals another,' Yhi replied. 'To put your spirit into the form of an animal would debase it; they would not respect you.'

'Then I will put a little part only into the animals,' said Baiame. He gave a small portion of his power of thought to birds, and insects, and reptiles, and fish, and to animals. They were governed by that part of thought which is known to man as instinct.

But Baiame was not yet satisfied.

'My whole mind must be put into something that has life and is worthy of the gift,' he said. 'I will need to make a new creation.'

From the processes of thought, the joining together of atoms and microscopic grains of dust, the forming of blood and sinews, cartilage and flesh, and the convolutions of the substance of the brain, he formed an animal that walked erect on two legs. It had hands that could fashion tools and weapons and the wit to use them; above all, it had a brain that could obey the impulses of the spirit; and so Man, who was greater than all other animals, was fashioned as a vessel for the mind-power of the Great Spirit.

This was done in secret. No other eye saw the making of Man, and the minutes of eternity went by in the last great act of creation. The world became dark and sorrowful at the absence of the Great Spirit. Floods ravaged the land. The animals took refuge in a cave high up in the mountains. From time to time one of them went to the entrance to see if the floods had subsided; but there was nothing to be seen except the emptiness of the land and the endless swirling of the waters under a sunless sky.

Goanna, wise among the reptiles, went to look for himself, and returned hurriedly.

'I have seen a round, shining light like the moon. It is resting outside the cave,' he announced.

'Nonsense!' said Eagle. 'Bahloo is in the sky.'

'I said it was *like* the moon. That is how it appears to me.'

Eagle went out. On his return everyone looked at him expectantly.

'It is a kangaroo,' Eagle said quickly. 'It has two bright eyes, so it is silly to say that it is like the moon. The eyes shine so brightly that their light pierced my body.'

'This is a strange thing,' said the animals. 'Goanna says it is like the moon, and Eagle says it is like a kangaroo. Which are we to believe? Crow, you are the cleverest of us all. You go out and look, and come back and tell us what this strange being is really like.'

Crow preened his feathers, but made no move until they pushed him forward. Then he squawked loudly and fluttered up into a crevice in the rock where none could touch him.

'Leave me alone,' he called fiercely. 'I am not interested. This is a thing that birds and animals should have nothing to do with. If we keep quiet it will probably go away.'

'If Crow is afraid, I'll go,' Mouse said bravely. He crept out on silent paws, but when he came back he could not speak. One after the other the birds and animals tiptoed to the entrance and looked at the strange being that stood there in the half light. There were many arguments, because the little part of Baiame's mind that was in each of them recognised a little part of the whole mind that was clothed in flesh outside the cave.

The unchanging night lasted for a period which could not be measured in sunrises and sunsets, which were but a paling and a brightening of the grey mist. The animals grew hungry. Eagle killed Rat and ate his body. It was the signal for widespread slaughter. Larger animals tore small ones to pieces and devoured their flesh. Baiame heard their tumult and left the mountain, saddened that the animals had discovered the pleasure that comes with the death of others.

As he went Yhi flooded the world with light. The remaining animals came out of the cave and gathered together on the hilltop. There on the pinnacle of the roof of the world they saw the Great Spirit revealed to them at last. Baiame stood before them in the form of Man, of Man who rules over all creation because he has the soul and intelligence of Baiame in a human body.

As he walked through the earth, the Man that was the thought-power of Baiame was lonely. Strange feelings surged through him, undiscovered desires. He needed a companion to share the wonder of the world, and he sought for one fruitlessly. He went to Kangaroo and Wombat, Snake and Lizard, Bird and Flying Fox, Fish and Eel, Insect and Earthworm, but in vain. He was kin to them because they loved the Great Spirit, but there was only a little part of Baiame's mind in each of them, and it was not enough to satisfy the hunger of Man's spirit.

He turned to trees, and to grasses, and to flowers. Their beauty intoxicated him, but they appealed only to his senses, for the eternal spirit of Baiame had not been conferred on them. The flaming flowers of the waratah, the golden glory of the wattle, the scented leaves and grey bark of the eucalypts were a delight to eyes and nose. He drew deep breaths of fresh perfume, but still his soul was not at rest.

In the evening he went to sleep near a grass yacca tree. All night he was troubled with strange dreams, in which his desires seemed to be on the point of fruition. When he woke again he found that Yhi had thrown her rays across the plain. They seemed to be concentrated on the tall flower stalk of the yacca tree. He gazed at it for a long while, until he was roused by the sound of heavy breathing. He looked round and was astonished to see that the whole animal creation had gathered together on the plain. In the air was a feeling of expectancy.

He looked back at the tree. It was changing. The flower stalk grew shorter and rounder. Limbs began to form, and with a shock Man realised that the tree was changing into a two-legged creature like himself.

But there was a difference. The limbs were smooth and soft, rounded breasts swelled before his eyes, there was a proud tilt to the shapely head. Man held out his hands to Woman. She clasped them and stepped gracefully across the grassy base of the tree. Man held her in his arms and together they surveyed the waiting world. The animals danced with delight and then ran off into the distance, satisfied that the loneliness of Man was ended.

The loneliness was ended; the duty and obligations of Man began. Woman came slowly to full life and communion with her husband. He hunted food for her. He sought shelter for her. He showed her love and tenderness, which are the fruits of the spirit. He taught her the names of birds and animals and their ways. She learned to love him, and to work for him, to be the other part of him that he needed for the satisfying of his longings and needs.

Baiame smiled. 'When I show myself to the little things I have created,' he mused, 'I shall be well content to show myself in the form of a Man!'

The Gift of Flowers

Baiame remained for a long while on earth as a man. He loved Tya, the world which, it is said, was once a piece of the sun itself. He made his home in a mountain, talking with the animals and the men and women whom he had created. There was communion of spirit between them, for the period of rest after the labours of creation were a refreshment to the Great Spirit. Day after day Yhi smiled at him as she moved across the vault of the sky, while round his earthly home the flowers bloomed in profusion.

One day he spoke to the men and women, and to the animals which crowded round him.

'The time has come for me to leave you, my children. While the earth was young you needed me, but now you are fully grown. It is better that you live by yourselves.'

A low moan went up, but he smiled and said, 'Do not be sad. Little children have no real minds of their own. When I am gone, and only then, you will learn to take your proper places in the world. If I were to remain here for ever you would come to me with all your troubles, and you would never learn to stand up for yourselves. But do not fear. Even though I shall return to my true home in the sky, in the bright patch of the Milky Way, I shall still be your Father Spirit. When you really need me, I shall be with you. Sometimes I shall return to earth, and then I shall take the form of a man so that you will recognise me.'

The animals dispersed slowly, but the men and women lingered. They had delighted in the flowers which grew so profusely round the mountain of Baiame and were loth to leave the many-coloured carpet with the sweet perfume. They lay on the carpet during the long nights looking up at the Milky Way, imagining that they could still see the Great Spirit.

A vague unease disturbed their minds. They could not tell what it was until a woman cried out, 'The flowers are gone!'

It was true. Men and women had understood Baiame's last message, and even animals, in whom Baiame had planted a little of his mind, knew that the Great Spirit had not left them for ever; but the flowers had no minds. All they knew was that the Father-Spirit was no longer with them, and that Yhi, the sun goddess, was far away.

'He has left us,' they murmured. Their drooping leaves and petals fell to the ground, and one by one they died.

'Look!' the woman cried again. 'There are no flowers left anywhere!'

As far as the eye could reach the earth was bare and brown. The circle of dead and dying plants was spreading through the whole world. Death of flowers raced ahead of the searching women, and all the raindrops sent by the spirits of the sky, and all the smiles of Yhi could not arrest it.

The air was filled with the black bodies of the bees as they flew frantically from one dead plant to another in search of honey.

'Now we shall have no honey,' the women cried. 'There is only the sweet gum of the trees that Baiame left, but they are his and we may not touch them.'

Even while they were speaking, trees grew up round them, and down their trunks flowed a clear liquid that quickly hardened. One woman, more venturesome than the rest, scraped some off with her finger and put it in her mouth.

'It is sweet,' she cried. 'Baiame has seen our plight and sent this food to us. These are not his sacred trees, which we would never touch. Come and eat.'

So their hunger was appeased, and they knew that Baiame still cared for them. Yet generation after generation was born and died, and still there were no flowers in the world. They were only a memory to the oldest people, a story that was told and scarcely believed by those who had been born long after the Death of Flowers. The stories grew with the telling, but no matter how fertile the imaginations of the tellers, the imagination could not equal the reality.

High in his starry home Baiame felt sorry for the descendants of his creation. He put into their minds a longing they could not resist. Gradually some of the men left their own camp grounds and gathered together at the foot of the mountain where Baiame had once lived as a man. They felt as though they were being drawn by invisible cords, up the endless slopes of the mountain and into the vast depression which had been made when

Baiame lay down on the carpet of flowers. And there was Baiame himself, holding out his hands, gathering them to himself as a hen gathers her chickens, and lifting them up to the starry sky.

'Come and see my home, little children,' he said in a deep voice that reverberated through he heavens and set the stars dancing in their courses.

He set them down on a cloud, and a great sigh echoed through the Milky Way, because as far as they could see there was a glowing carpet of colour, brighter than any rainbow, and with all the colours of the great bow they had seen after rain.

'The stories you have heard were true,' Baiame said. 'Once earth was covered with flowers like these, but never again. Yet my heart is sorrowful for you, and for your friends who will never see this sight. Gather armfuls of flowers now and take them back to earth with you. Take as many as you can. They will fruit and their seeds will take root, to gladden the hearts of you and your children and your children's children for ever.'

The gentle hand set them down again on the solid ground. Dropping flowers as they went, they ran to their own tribes, and scattered the largesse that the Father Spirit had given them. It could not be expected that the flowers would bloom as they did in the days of Baiame, in the Dreamtime; but never again will Earth be without flowers while the Great Spirit continues to watch over his people.

 ## The Plague of Insects

While he remained on Tya, the earth, Baiame let his imagination run riot. He fashioned mountains, covering them with trees and spreading a blue mist over them; he delighted in sending water spinning and laughing down their sides; he lined the banks with fragile plants that drank from the streams and bent over them in gratitude; at other times he swept his hand across the land and smoothed it into mallee-covered plains and sandy desert wastes. Tya grew and took form in his skilful fingers. Above it the pellucid wonder of the sky changed in colour from earliest dawn, when the stars winked out, to the brazen blue of midday, and the soft veils of evening.

As the sun rose in the mornings he looked at his handiwork, at the swaying trees and moving water, and he breathed soft winds across it, sending a million plants dancing with joy.

But like a wind on the embers of a camp fire, the jealousy of Marmoo, the Spirit of Evil, was also fanned to flame.

'Baiame's heart is too full of pride,' said Marmoo to his wife. 'Anyone could make a world out of Tya; but Baiame's vanity will be his downfall.'

'What can you do?' she asked. 'You have not tried to make a world for yourself.'

'I can do something better than that. I will spoil his precious world for him.'

'How?'

'You will see,' he said knowingly, and strode off into the dark forest where none could see him. In secrecy he made the insect tribe—beetles, flies, bugs, snails, worms, and a thousand other tiny creatures that crawled, and burrowed, and flew. There are tribes who say that the sun goddess Yhi brought to life all the animals, and birds, and insects that Baiame had created, but this is a story of Marmoo and his wickedness that is told by other camp fires.

For an endless time Marmoo laboured, breathing life into them, and sending them out of the forest in swarms. The sky was dark with flying insects, the ground became a heaving, crawling mass, and still Marmoo went on with his work.

The insects became a devouring host spreading out from the dark forest. They ate the grass, they bit the leaves from the trees. No plant was safe from them. The earth grew bare and ugly, the scent of flowers was replaced by the noxious smell of the plagues that devoured the living things that Baiame had made. Even the music of streams and waterfalls was drowned by the whirr of wings and the clashing jaws of the insect tribe.

Looking down with pride from his mountain home, Baiame saw the brown tide rolling over the plains and swarming up the foothills. The fair land he had made was being eaten up by the ravening hosts of Marmoo.

The Great Spirit was furious that his fair land should be so wantonly destroyed, but he felt he could get rid of the plague. He knew that it had been sent by Marmoo. Calling up one of the stronger winds, he sat down again to watch the dispersal of the insect swarms.

The wind whistled shrilly over the plain, but the insects clung with clawed feet to the tree trunks, or burrowed into the soil. Before the day was done Baiame knew that he would need help from his fellow spirits. He travelled quickly to the home of Nungeena, who lived in a waterfall hidden in a fertile valley in the mountains.

'Come with me and see what has happened to the beautiful land I made,' he said.

Nungeena was appalled at the sight.

'Your valley, too, will soon be like this,' Baiame warned her. 'The plague is coming closer. Unless you help me, your stream will be choked with creeping, crawling, slimy things, and there will be no place for you to live.'

Nungeena acted swiftly. She called her attendant spirits to her and asked them, 'What have you seen as you came to me?'

The spirits sighed. 'We have seen insects everywhere. The whole earth is being eaten up by them, Mother. What can we do to stop them?'

The Mother Spirit smiled. 'I have a plan,' she said, 'but you must help me.'

Her fingers flashed quickly in the sunshine, lifting colour from the flowers, weaving an intricate pattern in the air. When it was finished they saw the graceful form of a lyre bird standing in front of her.

'What is this, Mother?' they asked.

'It is a lyre bird. Look!'

She waved her hand again and the lyre bird moved, spreading its tail for all the spirits to admire. It flapped its wings and circled Nungeena.

'Wonderful!' cried the spirits. 'But how can it help us to get rid of the plague?'

'See for yourselves,' Nungeena replied. As they watched, the beautiful bird snapped at the advance guard of the insect tribe, which had already reached the Mother Spirit's resting place.

'We must work fast,' Nungeena said to her attendants. 'Birds are beautiful creatures, but it is more important that they should eat the insects quickly. We must set to work to make as many birds as we can. To work!'

Nungeena made other birds, and each one was different. The other spirits copied her as well as they could.

The younger spirits were clumsy. They made ugly-looking birds like the magpie and the butcher-bird but even these, as soon as they were made, began to snap up the insects.

The spirits who came from the watery regions of the world made birds that could swim and wade in the swamps and rivers. These began to eat the insects that were flying over the stream.

The spirits of the coastal lands were made gulls, and though these graceful birds are more fond of fish, they too joined in the great insect feast.

The night spirits who put the flowers to sleep made the mopokes and the nightjars.

The swiftest of the spirits made the fantails, the swallows, and the fly-catchers, and the air was filled with the snapping of their beaks.

The little spirits that spent their lives among the flowers fashioned robins, wrens, and mistletoe birds.

When they were all made the air was full of the sound and movement of wings. Baiame was delighted.

'They are so beautiful that they must have voices to match,' he said, and to each he gave the songs that have since rung through the bush and valleys, and across the plains of Tya. The harsh call of the crow and the raucous laughter of the kookaburra drowned the other sounds.

'Do you call that beautiful?' Nungeena asked incredulously.

'It is a pleasant sound in my ears,' Baiame retorted. He turned to the birds who by this time had eaten all the insects that had ventured into the valley of the Mother Spirit.

'Go forth and destroy the hordes of Marmoo,' he ordered.

Still singing, they circled round him and then fanned out like the spokes of a wheel, flying ever further away until they met fresh insect swarms that were denuding the earth of its vegetation. What a feast day for the birds! Never since have they been so fully fed; but they are always hoping that Marmoo will send them another bounteous harvest.

 The First Initiation Ceremony

The first corroboree and initiation ceremony the world has ever known was held at Googoorewon, the place of trees, while Baiame was still living on earth, and animals were still men.

The Great Spirit, who at that time had appeared to the tribes of men as a wirinun or medicine man, called his people together from their distant hunting grounds. Many tribes were there as the representatives of the animal world. There were the Wahn, the Crows; Du-mer, the Brown Pigeons; Baiamul, the Black Swans; Madhi, the Dogs; and many others.

As tribe after tribe came to the place Baiame had chosen for them, the excitement increased. Old friends greeted each other and inquired anxiously if anyone knew the purpose of the meeting, but none could read the mind of Baiame. The expectation, mingled a little with fear, increased hourly.

Yet it was a joyous occasion. Gifts were exchanged, marriage contracts were arranged, and those who had brought valuable possessions bartered them for others. There was dancing and singing every night until the fires burned low, and men and women could scarcely keep awake.

After several days Baiame summoned the men and addressed them as he stood outside his wurley.

'It is good for you to enjoy yourselves,' he told them, 'but now the serious business must begin. The real purpose of our meeting together in this place is to prepare the young men for manhood. You are men. You know what must be done because I have implanted these thoughts in your mind. First you must make a bora ground. Then the bullroarers will sound, the boys will leave their mothers, and you who are older will accept the responsibility of training them.'

The men spent several days clearing the ground, earthing up the protecting walls, and cutting a path through the scrub. Most of them worked quickly and silently, as tried warriors should do, but they were interrupted all the time by the senseless chatter and laughter of the Madhi tribe. Little notice was taken of them at first, for they were well known to be empty-headed. It was thought that when the bora ground began to take shape in the scrub the Madhi would be overawed by the solemnity of the coming rites. Occasionally a wirinun appealed to them to be quiet and help with the work; but they took no notice.

After a while threatening looks were cast at them, and the wirinuns warned them that if they would not be silent, the Great Spirit would be angry with them. The Madhis laughed contemptuously. They swaggered round the workmen making insulting remarks, criticising what was being done, and making rude gestures at the medicine men.

Baiame had been observing them closely. He had said nothing because he thought they stood in awe of the wirinuns. He believed that when the time of initiation drew near they would realise that as fully grown and tested men they must set an example to the boys. When it was evident that their bad manners and impudent behaviour were getting worse and worse, he decided that the time had come to punish them, for it was essential that the tribes should be protected and the initiates taken safely through their ordeal. He strode into their midst and spoke so loudly and sternly that they all stopped to listen.

'I am grieved at the behaviour of the Madhi,' the great wirinun said. 'My people live happily because they obey the laws I have made for them. Yet you, the Madhi, are proud and rebellious. You have not listened to the wise men; you are making a mockery of this solemn occasion. Very well:

you may go on laughing and howling to your hearts' content. No longer will I dignify you with the name or appearance of men. Go your way, Madhi, and continue your howling.'

One by one the Madhi dropped on all fours. Hair grew thickly over their bodies, their arms changed to legs, their hands and feet to paws. They tried to call out to Baiame and tell him they were sorry for what they had done. It was too late. No words but barking and howling noises came out of their mouths. They were scared by their own noise and fled yelping into the scrub. The noise died away in the distance.

Everyone was now afraid of Baiame. They had known him only as a friend. Now he had shown himself as a wirinun who would not be trifled with. In the shelter of the wurleys and around the camp fires that night the story of the day's events was told over and over again.

Next morning, when Baiame walked into the circle where a group of women was gathered, they fell silent and looked at him apprehensively.

'Why are you not grinding seeds for flour?' he asked.

No one replied.

'Come,' said Baiame jestingly. 'I am not going to eat you, but by tonight I will be hungry. If the cakes are not ready, anything may happen.'

One of the older women plucked up courage to speak.

'Oh sir, do not think us idle. A strange thing has happened. Our grinding stones have left us.'

Baiame roared with laughter.

'I have heard of women leaving grinding stones, but never of grinding stones leaving of their own accord. Can't you think of a better story to tell than that?'

'It is true, sir,' she insisted. 'There is not one left in the camp.'

Baiame looked round about.

'Certainly they are not here,' he admitted, 'but that does not mean that they grew legs and walked away. I expect you lent them to the Du-mer?'

'No, no, no, we did not,' came a chorus of voices.

'Yes, yes, yes, you did. Go and get them at once.'

Frightened by the fate of the Madhis, the women did not argue. They knew they had not lent the stones to the Brown Pigeons; still, they went from one group to another asking, 'Have you seen our grinding stones?' but the answer was always 'No.'

'Listen!' cried one of the girls. 'What is that noise?'

They stopped and heard a peculiar drumming noise overhead.

'The Wunda! The spirits are here!' cried a voice.

They ran back as quickly as they could and told Baiame that they had heard the Wunda.

The wirinun stroked his beard and said thoughtfully, 'Perhaps I have done you an injustice. Let us go and visit the Du-mer and see for ourselves.'

He took up his magic weapons and went towards the camp of the Du-mer women, followed at a respectful distance by the other women. The Du-mer camp was deserted, but one woman, sharper-eyed than the others, saw a grinding stone gliding between the bushes. Baiame hurried after it, still followed by the women, while overhead the drumming of the Wunda went on monotonously.

'It is being carried by a Wunda whom we cannot see,' Baiame said.

They broke through a scrub and an astonishing sight met their eyes. Hundreds of grinding stones were streaming across the bare plain, and running after them were the Du-mer women. As they looked the Du-mers were changed into Brown Pigeons which flapped their wings and flew towards the bush.

'Follow! Follow!' cried Baiame. Over streams and across country they ran. But the stones were carried faster than they could run and were lost to sight in the distance. Yet Baiame urged the women on.

'Look!' he said at last. 'This is where the chase ends.'

A stony mountain rose from the open plain. It was Mount Dirangibirra. When they reached it they found it was composed entirely of grinding stones. Ever since that day the tribes who want the best stones for grinding always go to Mount Dirangibirra to secure them.

While the weird noise of the bullroarers rose and fell, the women huddled together in camp, fearful of the mysteries that may be attended only by men. The boys had been taken away by their guardians and only the women and children were left.

On the bora ground the young men summoned to their defence the fortitude that had been gained through long years of privation, pain, and loneliness. There had been times when they were driven to the very edge of madness and hysteria, but they were as nothing to the tests they now had to endure. They remembered the freezing, fireless cold of night and the strange noises that had come out of the darkness when the elder brothers had driven them away from their camps; the long day's hunting, the first thrill of seeing a stone-tipped spear sink into their prey, the thirsty trek back to the camp, the pride with which they had thrown the kill on the ground for all to admire, the shattering realisation that others would eat it while they, the hunters, were forced to go hungry. These experiences had befallen them when they were young and in their innocence they had thought that the endurance of such tests would bring with them the privileges of manhood.

But Baiame had instructed his wirinuns wisely.

'My children must be strong,' he told them. 'Strong to father sons, to care for their women, to overcome appetite and pain and fear. They must learn the wisdom of the tribes, the mystery of water and all the stars of heaven, of winds that blow, the flight of the bee to its honey store, the food that is hidden under the earth, the seeing eye that can follow the light-footed trail of the kangaroo rat over stony ground. Teach them!'

Through blackened, bleeding lips the young men tried to follow the chanting of the wirinuns. The initiates were stretched out on the hot sand while ants crawled on their bare skin, and investigated the clay patterns painted on their bodies. The blood trickled slowly across their thighs and was licked up by the thirsty soil. No food or water had been given to them for many days, and the blood roared in their ears like thunder. Memory was blotted out as the old lore was chanted by the wirinuns. The thunder changed to the sound of a waterfall as the churingas whirled on and on. If one of the young men succumbed to fatigue his head was jerked back and a fresh gash reminded him that he had slackened the grasp of his mind.

Through the nights of spring the singing, the telling, the whispering, the endless whirring of the churingas kept on—until early one morning, when the bushes looked like men crouching in the dim light, the last act was performed. The elder brothers sat on their bodies until their ribs cracked in the cave of their chests and the breath was pressed out of their lungs, while the wirinuns, with sharp flints and heavy pounding stones, knocked out their front teeth.

The sound of the churingas died away, and in the hush of dawn the young men stood up, their eyes shining, to face the world with the experience and all the pride of men.

Weeks had passed slowly by, and presently the mothers looked forward to seeing their sons again. They would admire them as they proudly took their place with the seasoned hunters and warriors. Privately, when no one was looking, they would weep over the smashed teeth and gashed bodies of the men who such a short while before had been little boys. They did not want to meet them at the bora ground, so they packed their few possessions and began the long march back to their own tribal lands.

One day a middle-aged woman walked into the camp and fell in front of them, beating her breast and crying, 'You have deserted me. Shame on you! May you all be mothers of twins!'

'What is the matter? What is wrong with you?' they asked, gathering round her.

'I could not keep up with you,' she sobbed. 'My children were many, and they were small. They grew tired. The quicker you walked, the more slowly they went. Not one of you looked back. Not one of you would help. We could not find the water holes, and one by one my children died and now not one is left to me.'

She scrambled to her feet, her eyes glaring, and cursed them.

'You would not wait for us. You were in too much of a hurry to get here. You did not care that you had killed my children. You are here now, and here you will remain. Goo gool gai ya! Turn into trees—every one of you!'

She fell backwards, her tongue protruding from her mouth, with her sightless eyes turned upwards. The women tried to reach her, but their feet were rooted to the ground. As they bent over her their outstretched arms turned into branches, their fingers into twigs and leaves, their legs and bodies into tree trunks. The wind rustled through them and they wailed in agony.

Other tribes of women heard the unusual noise and rushed to them to see what was happening. As they came close they were changed into other shapes—the Baiamuls to Black Swans, the Ooboons to Blue-tongued Lizards sliding cross the grass. The Du-mers flew overhead cooing with the sound that the Wundas had made when they stole the grinding stones. And from the dead body of Millin-nulu-nubba, the bereaved mother, came the little bird Millin-nulu-nubba who keeps on crying, 'Goo gool gai ya! Turn into trees!'

Back at the bora ground Baiame welcomed the young men who had conquered appetite, pain, and fear.

'Welcome,' said the wise old wirinun. 'You are all men now. The women have started on their homeward way. We shall follow. They are burdened by their children, and we shall quickly catch them up.'

The trail was easy to follow. Baiame's own dog raced ahead and reached the glade where the trees, that had so lately been women, bent their heads towards the ground. Animals scuttled out of her way. The dog lay down under a bush and gave birth to pups, which had the bodies of dogs and the heads of porcupines. They were so fierce that no one dare go near them. Men call them the Eer-moonans, the long-toothed monsters of the dark shades, who tear travellers limb from limb with their sharp teeth.

Baiame went sadly back to his home in the mountains. The greatest initiation ceremony ever known was ended; but women had been turned into trees, men to dogs, whole tribes to reptiles and birds, and even his own dog had left him and given birth to monsters.

But Baiame is old and wise. From evil comes good; and he knew that when the sharp memories of the initiation were over, the world would be richer because of the presence of the plants and animals that had come from his great bora.

 ## The Wives of Baiame

Before leaving the world to go to his home in the Milky Way, Baiame climbed the ladder of stone steps to the summit of Mount Oobi-oobi, whose peak is in Bullima. There, when he made his last departure, his wives were attached to a crystal rock, as a remembrance of the time when Baiame looked and spoke as a man and walked upon the earth.

Long before their petrification, Birra-nulu and Kunnan-beili, the women chosen to be his wives, were young and foolish. He could never trust them out of his sight for long.

'I want you to be careful and listen to what I am about to say,' he told them one day. 'I am going out to search for honey. While I am away, take your digging-sticks and get some yams, and as many frogs as you can find. Take them to the spring at Coorigil and wait for me there. But whatever you do, don't bathe in the spring. The water at that place is only for drinking.'

He opened his hand and a bee flew out, trailing a tuft of white down. The Great Spirit ran after it and was soon lost to sight.

'He'll be gone a long time,' said Birra-nulu. 'He'll never give up till the bee has reached its home in a tree. Let's get to work, and then perhaps we can have some fun while he's away.'

They worked so quickly that in a short time their bags were full of food, and this they carried to the spring.

'The water looks cool, and I am hot. What would you do if you were me?' Kunnan-beili asked.

'I would go for a swim. What would you do if you were me, Kunnan-beili?'

'I would go for a swim.'

They looked at each other and burst out laughing.

'Old Baiame warned us not to go, but sometimes I think he's just a silly old man who doesn't understand what girls are like. Let's go!'

They took off their girdles and jumped into the spring, shouting with delight at the shock of the cold water. Deep down in the spring two menacing shapes began to stir. Silently they swam up through the clear water, unnoticed by the young women. Two huge mouths gaped wide and the jaws of the Kurrias, the crocodile guardians of the pool, closed over them. At one moment the laughter of the girls filled the glade, then silence fell as the birds stopped singing, and even the gentle breeze died away. Birds and animals looked in horror at the eddies on the surface of the pool, and the grim shapes that vanished in its depths.

The Kurrias did not sink to the bottom. They knew that the bodies of the women in their bellies were the wives of Baiame, and their only thought was to escape before the god discovered what had happened to them. Halfway down the bore of the spring was a channel which led to the Narran river. They crawled along the narrow passage, pushing the water in front of them. Down the Narran river they sped. The water heaped itself in front of their bodies in a wave that spread over the banks and surged against the tree trunks, leaving the bed of the river empty behind them.

Baiame had gathered his supply of honey. He went quickly to the Coorigil spring, wondering what mischief his women might have been getting up to during his absence. He called out to them, but there was no answer. He heard the croaking of frogs in the dilly bags which had been placed in the shade of the trees, and on the edge of the spring he saw their girdles, left where they had thrown them when they went to bathe.

He walked to the edge and saw that the surface of the pool was far below its usual level. The blood beat in his temples and his hands tightened over his weapons when he realised that the women had disobeyed him and had been swallowed by the Kurrias. He scrambled down the steep bank, and hope returned when he saw the black tunnel through the rock.

Crouching on hands and knees, he crawled along it and came out on the empty river bed. He knew that the crocodiles would move slowly, dragged down by the weight of Birra-nulu and Kunnan-beili. The dry river bed twisted and turned in front of him, but Baiame climbed on to the bank and strode across country to where he could see a distant gleam of silver, which indicated that the Kurrias were still travelling downstream. The pebbles slipped and slid down the river bank as he rushed onwards, forming the ridges that now lead towards the Narran River.

He came to a place where the river spread out into a shallow lake, and sat down to wait. Presently he saw a towering wave coming rapidly towards him. It spread over the lake and the Kurrias came ashore at the very spot where he was waiting. He sprang to his feet and before they had time to rush him, he had fitted a spear to his woomera and pierced one of them through the head, pinning it to the ground. The other he struck with his nullanulla, stunning it for a moment. Avoiding their lashing tails he cut off their heads and slit their bellies with his flint knife.

The bodies of his wives rolled out on the bank. They lay still, covered with thick slime. Now Baiame searched until he found a nest of red ants. He gathered a quantity of them and placed them on the girls' bodies, where they ran to and fro, licking up the coat of slime until their skins shone in the sunlight. Roused by the tickling of many tiny feet and the bites of many ants, the young women stirred, sat up, and climbed shakily to their feet.

They hung their heads in shame when they saw their husband looking at them.

'We are sorry. We were very foolish,' they said.

Baiame smiled at them. He was always tolerant with his light-headed wives.

'Your adventure has ended happily,' he said. 'Maybe it will teach you to listen to your husband another time. There is always a reason for the orders I give you. If it had not been for me you would still be lying inside the Kurrias, and your bodies would have been eaten away by the juices of their bellies. Will you promise me never to go swimming in any pool or billabong or river without my permission?'

'We will! We will!' answered Birra-nulu and Kunnan-beili.

 ## Baiame and the Land of Women

At the end of the world, beyond the mountain where Baiame the Great Spirit lived, there was once a land inhabited only by women. These women were famous for their skill in making weapons—spears, boomerangs, and nullanullas. They traded them with men for meat and possum skins which they needed for food and warmth, because there were no animals on the other side of Baiame's mountain. Hunters were equally glad to trade with them, for the weapons that the women made were the finest in the world.

It was difficult to reach the land of women. A vast waterless plain had to be traversed. Then the traveller could proceed no further because his way was barred by a deep lake. No one was allowed to cross it. The traveller would place his load of meat and skins on the bank and retire. When he was out of sight the women would paddle across the lake in their canoes and exchange the gifts for weapons. Yet in spite of the high cost and heavy labour, men were ready to go to such lengths for the sake of the beautiful weapons that conferred honour and dignity on those who owned them.

But there are always rebels who will not conform to the pattern set by others. Such a man was Wurrunah.

'It is ridiculous that men should be content to accept what women are prepared to give them,' he complained to his brothers. 'After all, they are only women, and men should be their masters. If no one else will do it, I will show them how they ought to be treated.'

'How can you possibly do this?' they asked him. 'No one is allowed to cross the lake. We shall not be able to approach them.'

Wurrunah laughed scornfully.

'Men are always more clever than women,' he replied. 'Women make them weak by their wiles; but if a man is strong and determined he will always win. I'll tell you what we shall do.

'First, we must enlist the help of a number of trusty men. We will take no food, no rugs. Instead each man will bring with him a live animal. It doesn't matter what it is so long as it is alive.'

'What will we do with the animals?'

'Never mind. You must trust me. I shall tell you what to do when we get there.'

With some difficulty a band of men was gathered together and a curious procession set out across the sun-scorched plain. Wurrunah was in the lead, followed by his brothers. After them came a number of men, each carrying a live animal, well-roped and slung across his back.

When at length they reached the edge of the lake, Wurrunah gave his instructions.

'First of all I will turn my two brothers into white swans. They will swim across the lake. The women will notice them and, as they have never seen any birds except Wahn, and Mullian who is Baiame's messenger, they will launch their canoes and try to catch the birds. In the meantime I will go round the lake. When I reach the women's camp I will gather up their complete stock of weapons. This is sure to bring the women back in a hurry. As soon as I see them approaching, I will shout. When I have given the signal I want you to release your animals. The attention of the women will be distracted by them, and while they are going back and chasing the animals, I will make my escape. Then we shall meet and I shall distribute the weapons among you.'

Wurrunah conjured up his most powerful magic. His brothers were changed into two beautiful white swans which glided across the calm lake waters. The women, amazed at the sight, launched their canoes and set off in pursuit.

Wurrunah crept up to the deserted camp and tied all the weapons he could find into a bundle, and placed them on his back. As he left the camp, doubled up under his load, the women saw him. They abandoned the chase of the white swans and paddled furiously towards the shore. Wurrunah gave a loud shout, and his men released the animals. Never had the women seen such a sight before. They leaped ashore and ran in all directions trying to capture them. In the confusion Wurrunah made his escape and passed the weapons over to his followers.

They felt no further allegiance towards him. Each man took his newly-gained, treasured possession and hurried away to the plain and the long journey back to his home. But Wurrunah was elated with his success. He had conquered the redoubtable women, and felt power flowing through his body. He lifted his eyes up to the summit of the lofty mountain where it was said that the Great Spirit lived, and in a mood of defiance began to climb the sacred slopes. He had not gone far before black thunderclouds rolled across the peak, and vivid shafts of lightning lit the gloom. One spear-point of light stabbed down the mountain side and struck his body. Wurrunah fell to earth, bruised and defenceless. The newly-won power ebbed away. The magic departed from him, and there was none left to turn his brothers back to their true form. Sobbing for breath, he turned his footsteps towards the plain.

As he plodded across it, Eagle-hawk soared far above him. Mullian had seen the clouds gathering and knew that his master had called him. His attention was caught by two white dots floating on the lake far beneath. He swooped down and was enraged to find that Baiame's preserves had been invaded by the swans. He attacked them fiercely, tearing out their feathers until they drifted across the water in a white cloud.

The swan brothers cried out to their brother for help. Wurrunah heard them from far away, but was powerless. He could only stand and wring his hands. Yet help was close at hand. The mischievous crows, the birds called

Wahn, had made their nests in the sacred mountain, under the very beaks of their enemies the Eagle-hawks. They heard the despairing cries of the swans as they sank lower in the water, and took pity on them. They too were rebels against the might of Baiame. They plucked the black feathers from their plumage and scattered them over the swans until they were warm again, and able to swim ashore.

Baiame looked down and was amused at their temerity, and touched by their kindness to the swans; as a reward he allowed the swans to live and decreed that all the swans of Australia would have black feathers instead of white.

Part II

Legends of Sun, Moon and Stars

 Why Kookaburra Laughs at Dawn

Some time when the world was young, birds and animals had grown to an enormous size. They were as big as mountains and they lived in darkness that was lit only by the dim light of the stars. The animals were quarrelsome, for it was difficult to find food enough to support their enormous bodies. Baiame had begun his acts of creation, but had not yet determined what form his people would take. These animals he had made were his first experiments.

The world was not a comfortable place in which gods could live. Baiame preferred to remain in his home in the Milky Way which he shared with another powerful spirit, whose name was Punjel. In the frosty realms of the sky it was cold, and every day the gods collected firewood, which they piled in a heap in front of their celestial wurley.

'Why do we gather all this wood but never set it alight?' Punjel asked plaintively.

'We have no fire. Fire is found only in the world below.'

'Then why don't we go down and get some for ourselves? I am cold.'

'You must remain cold for a while longer,' Baiame told him. 'The time will come. You cannot hasten the processes of creation.'

Punjel was prepared to argue, but his attention was attracted by an unusual sight. Both he and Baiame were able to see clearly in the half-light that enveloped the world. They saw that Eagle and Emu were fighting over the carcase of some animal. Emu managed to snatch it away from Eagle. He rushed towards his nest with the other bird hot in pursuit. Eagle's beak was stretched out and he was pulling the tail feathers from the fleeing bird. Emu did not dare to stay by the nest. He ran straight on into the dense undergrowth and was lost to sight. Eagle stopped, and began to walk back towards the Emu nest. He looked in and saw two white eggs glimmering in the darkness. He picked one of them out with his beak, transferred it to his claw, and with a wicked smile on his face, threw it up in the air with all his might.

Punjel had been watching closely. The egg soared upwards, higher and higher, and as it came closer to him it seemed to grow so large that it blotted out his view of the world. Instinctively Punjel put out his hand to catch it, but it slipped through his fingers and smashed against the wood pile outside the wurley. It broke into a thousand pieces, and the timber was splashed with white and gold. As the two great spirits watched, the shattered egg burst into flames, the wood was kindled, and as it had been stored for so long and was tinder-dry, it burned furiously. The gods drew near to warm their bodies.

Presently they looked down. The stars had paled before the intense glow of the fire, and the whole world was lit up by the flames. They drew their breath quickly at the sight. Never before had they seen such beauty. Mountain tops were touched with pure gold; trees were like a feathery green garment on the hillsides; silver streams and waterfalls adorned a land that shone in splendour. Even the arid plains were glowing with a thousand bright colours; while the clouds that drifted over the earth's face were gossamer veils that enhanced her loveliness.

'This is your doing, Baiame,' said Punjel. 'Under cover of darkness you have been making the world beautiful so that we may enjoy it forever.'

Baiame smiled: 'Not for us alone, Punjel. The huge animals of the darkness have had their day. Now it is time to people this world of mine with little animals, small birds and reptiles, even tiny insects that we can scarcely see, and to put silvery fish into the rivers and lakes.'

As he was speaking the fire began to die down, and some of the beauty was concealed again.

'What is the use of making such a world if no one is able to see it?' Punjel asked.

'Now that we have the gift of fire in the heavens,' Baiame replied, 'we will never let it go out. At night it will die down till no one can see it, but in the morning I shall light it again. Men will call it the sun, but we know that it is a new woodpile burning brightly to waken all living things from sleep.'

'What is sleep?' asked Punjel.

'Sleep is a gentle spirit that closes men's eyes and soothes the thoughts out of their heads. It is a time of resting. Living things need sleep.'

'Do you mean that they are dead?'

'No, no. It is hard to tell you, because you do not know it, but sleep is a not-living that keeps men alive.'

Punjel shook his head in a puzzled fashion. 'I don't understand, Baiame,' he said. 'If you say it is good, it must be good. But if men are living yet not living, and their eyes are closed, they will not know when the fire is lit, and they will go on and on in this thing that you call sleep, which is like death.'

'They will open their eyes to the fire each day,' Baiame assured him. 'I shall hang a bright star in the east, and by that they will know that the fire is to be lit again, and that light is coming back to the world.'

'How can they know when the star is there, if their eyes are shut?'

'There will be a noise that will wake them when the star shines.'

'What kind of noise? Who will make it?'

'That is for you to find out, Punjel. Since you are so concerned lest my little ones should not wake up each day, you must try to find a way of letting them know.'

Punjel went back into his wurley, and tried to think. 'I could carry stones up to the Milky Way and drop them on the earth,' he thought, 'but then they might hurt Baiame's people when they fell. Anyway, that would not be a happy sound to wake everyone. They might be afraid.'

After thinking for a long time, he went down to earth and wandered through the bush. He listened to the branches of trees creaking together in the wind, to water trickling over stones, to the thudding of the paws of animals on the ground; but none of these things satisfied him.

Then he heard a sound of laughter, and went to see what it was. He found Kookaburra perched on the branch of a tree, laughing happily to himself.

'Kookaburra!' he cried, 'that is just the sound I want. Can you laugh louder than that?'

Kookaburra opened his beak wide and let out such a peal of laughter that Punjel had to block his ears to stop being deafened.

'Wonderful!' he cried again. 'Everyone will be able to hear that noise in the farthest corners of the world. Kookaburra, before the sky fire is lit each morning Baiame will hang a star in the eastern sky. Will you watch for it, and laugh your happy laugh when you see it?'

'Of course I will,' said Kookaburra. 'I am happiest when I am laughing.'

Punjel flew up to the sky, and told Baiame what he had done.

'Good!' said the Great Spirit. 'When I put the morning star in the east, listen and tell me whether you can hear Kookaburra giving the dawn call.'

But there was no need for him to ask Punjel to listen. He could hear it himself, like everyone else except those who are stone deaf.

 ## The Blue Fish and the Moon

Who can tell how the moon was made? How did he first set out on his long journey across the sky? Did Bahloo the Moon God live in the Dreamtime with Baiame and Yhi and all the spirits of the heavens? Who can tell?

But there is a tale that is told of Nullandi, the Happy Man, and Loolo, the Miserable Man, who both lived before the moon shone, when the nights were dark and friendless.

'My heart is like the dark,' Loolo said to his wife, as they lay in the shelter of the fence and huddled close to the fire to keep the heat in their bodies. 'The night is unfriendly. When we die our spirits will walk through an unending night of darkness, the winds will blow through the empty spaces of that night, and they will shrivel up and die, and we shall be no more.'

His only answer was the sobbing of his wife as she buried her head in her arms.

From Nullandi's fire came sounds of laughter.

'See the darkness!' he said. 'It rests our eyes after the fierce light of the sun by day.'

'You are foolish, husband,' his wife replied. 'How can we see the darkness? There is nothing to see. It is as though we were to place our hands over our closed eyes.'

'That is because you do not look,' Nullandi said. 'Look into the fire, wife. Look into the fire, children. See the flames leaping there. Keep on looking. Now look into the dark. What do you see now?'

'We see flames in the darkness,' they cried together. 'Why is that, Father? Are there many fires all over the world?'

'No, they are in your heads. It is more important that they should be there than in the world. Can you still see them?'

'They are growing dim, Father.'

'Then look up into the sky. What do you see there?'

'We see many many sparks up there. What fire do they come from?'

'They must be sparks from the fire that Baiame has lit. We cannot see it yet, but when dawn comes we will see its yellow glow.'

'But why is the sky covered with sparks, Father?'

'I cannot tell you that. You must wait till you are old men and women, and your spirits take the long trail to Bullima. Then you will learn many mysteries that only the spirits of the dead learn when they become alive for ever more. See, I will become Baiame for you.'

He took a log from the fire and waved it through the air so that it became a circle of flame, and the sparks flew out like living creatures.

'Do it again,' the children shouted when Nullandi threw it back on the fire.

'No,' their father said sternly. 'That was just a kind of joking and I should not have done it, because no man can be like Baiame. Now go to sleep and in the morning the warmth of his fire will wake you to a wonderful world of light and colour.'

'What were you laughing at last night?' said Loolo. 'With your laughing and my wife crying I could not get to sleep.'

'Why was your wife crying?'

'I was telling her when death comes it will be like the darkness that falls after the sun has set.'

'That is not really so,' Nullandi said seriously. 'We cannot tell until the time comes, but I believe that death will be only for a little time ... so short that it will be like shutting our eyes and opening them again.'

'You are a foolish man,' Loolo said, and gave a croak that faintly resembled laughter. 'What do you think will happen to you?'

'I know that the Great Spirit has not made us for nothing, to be like a flower that blooms for a day and fades away, or like a twig that is consumed in the fierce heat of the fire. He has made us because we are his children, and when our time comes he will give us an even better place to live in than this beautiful world.'

'This is not a beautiful world. Often we are thirsty and hungry. We have to work all day to get food to keep our bodies alive. When it is all over that will be the end of us. The sparks will all go out, and only darkness will be left.'

Nullandi picked up his spear and began to sharpen the blade.

'You can think that if it makes you happy, Loolo. For me, I'm off to hunt for wallabies while my wife gets some waterlily roots for our evening meal. Listen to me: you are making your wife miserable with all your talk. If you want to be a blue fish at the bottom of the sea when you die, you can be a blue fish for all I care. But leave your wife alone and let her be happy.'

'You leave your wife alone too, Nullandi. Let her make up her own mind. What do you think will happen to you when your body lies dead on the plain and the dingoes come and eat your flesh?'

Nullandi thought for a while. 'I don't really know, Loolo. I am content to leave it all to Baiame. But I tell you this: if there are many people like you in the world who dread the dark, perhaps Baiame will make me a light to comfort them.'

The long years rolled by. Nullandi and Loolo grew old. When they had no strength left, they lay down and died, and Loolo became a blue fish which lived for a little while at the bottom of the sea. Then he was eaten by another fish and his bones lay on the muddy bed of the sea until they crumbled and fell to pieces. That was the end of Loolo.

But Nullandi the Happy Man went up into the sky, to the home of Baiame, where the Great Spirit turned him into the round and shining moon. Nullandi turned the darkness of the nights to silver light, and even when he waned and became as thin as a sliver of bark, men knew that he would grow again, just as their own spirits might die for a little while, and then come to life and live for ever.

So Nullandi the Happy Man became Bahloo, the cheerful God of the Moon.

Wahn and the Moon God

Wahn the Crow had long been envious of Bahloo, because the Moon God was the maker of baby girls.

'Let me help you. I'm very good at making babies,' Wahn begged him.

Bahloo was suspicious of his friend, and with good reason, for when at last he consented, reluctantly, because of the great number that were needed, Wahn produced babies which grew up to be noisy and quarrelsome. They inherited Crow's own disposition.

On one occasion the two baby-makers quarrelled. Wahn wanted to take the spirits of men and women who had died and put them back into the bodies of unborn babies.

'We cannot do that,' Bahloo protested. 'Every baby born into the world must fulfil its own destiny.'

'But think how wonderful it would be to give people a chance to live their lives all over again. They would learn by the mistakes they made the first time.'

'Nonsense, Wahn. You haven't thought about it properly. The good spirits have all gone to Bullima, and the others are having a bad time at the hands of the Eleanba Wunda. No one would want to inflict the lost spirits on poor little new-born babies.'

'Bahloo, you know very well that some spirits go and live in the bodies of living men and women. I know where to find them.'

'They won't go and live in the bodies of my babies,' Bahloo said firmly. 'If you don't forget the whole silly idea I won't let you help make my girl babies, ever.'

Wahn hopped off in a huff. While he was hunting for grubs a pleasant thought occurred to him. He hurried back to his friend.

'Forget what I said about the babies, Bahloo. Full bellies are more important than new ideas. I have found a tree with hundreds of grubs in the bark. You never saw anything like it in your life. I need your help.'

Wahn gave Bahloo his hooked stick and said, 'I've already got a bag full of them. It is your turn now. Take this hook and climb up the tree. I will stay down below and catch them as you throw them down to me.'

Relieved that Wahn had forgotten his peculiar ideas about babies, Bahloo climbed into the tree and began to fossick in the crevices of the bark with the hooked stick.

'Where are they? I can't find any,' he shouted.

'Higher up,' Wahn called to him. 'I've taken all the lower ones. You'll have to climb further into the branches.'

Bahloo climbed higher and found a plentiful supply of grubs, which he pulled out of their hiding places, and threw down to Wahn. Every time he caught one, Crow put it into his bag and breathed on the trunk of the tree. There was magic in his breath and the tree grew quickly, inching its way upwards. There were many grubs, and by the time Bahloo had gathered the last of them, the tree had lifted him far into the sky. He looked down. Wahn was so far away that he seemed like an ant on the ground. The Moon God cupped his hands and shouted, 'Where am I? What has happened?'

The only reply was a faint cackle of laughter from Wahn.

Bahloo remained in the sky for a long time, and while he was there, Yhi, the Sun Goddess fell in love with him. Bahloo knew all about her. She had many lovers and Bahloo would have nothing to do with her, but he had nowhere to run and hide except in the empty spaces of the sky. Sometimes he was eclipsed, but always he managed to escape.

Although Yhi will never be satisfied until she captures the Moon, the rejection of her advances has made her angry. Knowing that Bahloo's ambition was to return to earth, she instructed the spirits who hold up the edges of the sky to turn him back whenever he attempted to slide down to earth.

'If you let him escape,' she threatened them, 'I will take away the spirit who holds up the earth. It will sink down, down, down into darkness—and you will go with it.'

Bahloo became desperate. In his absence Wahn was having the time of his life, making babies by the hundred, every one of them noisy and quarrelsome. So Bahloo disguised himself as an emu and walked boldly past the spirits of the sky. It was night time. Back on earth, he crept inside his gunyah and whispered to his wives.

'Be quiet,' he said. 'It is Bahloo. I don't want my brothers to know that I am here. Have they been worrying you?'

The youngest wife giggled.

'We have seen a lot of them while you have been away.'

'I thought so,' Bahloo said grimly.

He went outside and brought in a log which was the home of a spirit called Mingga. He put it on the ground and told one of his wives to cover it with a possum skin so that it looked like a man sleeping on the floor.

'Now come with me,' he whispered.

They followed him outside and into the bush. He did not stop until he came to a place where they would not be likely to be discovered, and there they set up their camp.

Shortly after they had left, Bahloo's brothers crept expectantly into the deserted gunyah.

'Strange,' one of them whispered. 'The women are not here. But who is that, rolled up in the possum skin?'

'It must be Bahloo! He has come back,' another said. 'This is the chance we have been waiting for.'

He raised his club and brought it down with all his force on the end of the log where he thought Bahloo's head would be.

'That's the end of brother Bahloo,' he said, and kicked the log viciously.

He staggered back with an agonized shout and hopped about on one foot, nursing the other in his hands.

Another brother twitched the skin back and realised that they had all been tricked by the Moon God. They followed his trail, but Bahloo had changed back into an emu, and they were never able to find him again.

In the meantime Bahloo had settled down happily in his new camp, and continued his task of making female babies. After a while he was joined by his friend Bu-maya-mul, the Wood Lizard, who was responsible for creating boy babies. Bu-maya-mul had little regard for girl babies. He tried to change Bahloo's girl spirits into boys, but the Moon God stopped him, saying, 'I know you respect hunters and warriors, but after all, they need wives and daughters. Leave them alone.'

When a number of baby spirits were ready they gave them into the care of Walla-gudjail-uan, the spirit of birth, who has the responsibility of placing the unborn spirits where they will be found by the right mothers. The favourite food of Walla-gudjail-uan is mussels. Sometimes the baby spirits tease her by taking them away. Then she grows angry and threatens to hide them in places where they will never be found. Fortunately there is another spirit, Walla-guroon-buan, who takes pity on them and puts them in hollow trees, streams, and caves where they are sure to be found. These places are usually associated with different totems. When a woman comes close to the baby spirit's hiding place, she knows at once what its totem is.

The Moon God and the Birth Spirits had such an important part to play in the birth of the child that mothers and expectant mothers were careful not to offend them. If a woman stared at the moon, Bahloo would be annoyed and would send her twins. This was a disgrace that could not be lived down.

It was customary for mothers to stand under the drooping branches of a coolabah tree, which was a favourite hiding place for the baby spirits. A new baby is said to have a coolabah leaf in its mouth when it is born. This must be removed at once or the child will die, and its spirit will go back to the tree.

If the spirit baby was unable to find a mother, it wailed dismally until it was turned into a clump of mistletoe, the flowers of which were stained with the baby's blood.

But powerful though the Birth Spirits may be, it is Bahloo who is responsible for creating the bodies of all the girl babies in the world. If he is late in rising, the women say, 'Bahloo is busy making girl babies.' When he appears above the horizon he smiles down benignly on all women, for he knows he is the greatest influence in their lives.

 ## Waxing and Waning Moon

Moon was so fat that he was quite round. He was a good-natured man. He had only one sorrow which sometimes dimmed his face as though clouds were passing across it. Looking down at the earth he saw many attractive young women, and he longed to take one of them to cheer him on his lonely journey through the sky. Time after time he went to places where he could see camp fires burning cheerfully, and begged the girls to come with him, but they did not find him attractive. As soon as he appeared they ran away and hid in their gunyahs.

Moon would not give up, but he was so bright that he could be seen coming from a distance. The older people took to hiding all the eligible young women before Bahloo could reach their encampments.

One night he strolled down a valley where his light was hidden in the deep gorge. Coming round a bluff he saw two young women sitting by the bank of the river. They looked up at him with interest.

'It must be Bahloo, the Moon,' one whispered to the other. 'We have been warned against him, but I would like to see him.'

'So would I,' the other responded. 'Let us stay here and find out what he looks like. Everything looks so beautiful where he is walking.'

Moon quickened his footsteps when he saw that the girls did not run away. He broke into a shambling trot, at which they both began to laugh.

'His arms and legs are like twigs,' one of them gasped. 'Quick, let us take the canoes across the river before he catches us.'

They jumped into two canoes that were moored to the bank and paddled across.

Moon fell on his knees and pleaded with them.

'You did not run away at first. Why have you left me now? You are beautiful. I will do you no harm. If you come and live with me in the sky you shall be so happy.'

The only answer was their mocking laughter.

'It is good to live in the sky,' Bahloo persisted. 'Remember the Seven Sisters.'

The girls looked at one another and felt ashamed. Every young woman admired the Seven Sisters who were turned to an immortal constellation of stars.

'Perhaps we were cruel to him,' one girl said. 'Let us go back and help him.'

They paddled back to Bahloo's side of the river and jumped ashore.

'Choose which canoe you want. Then you can paddle to the other side and we will follow and bring the canoe back.'

Bahloo smiled to conceal his thoughts. It was not the canoes he wanted but the young women themselves.

'Alas, I have not learned to paddle,' he said. 'Get into the canoe with me and show me what I should do.'

'You get in, Bahloo,' one of them said. 'You are so fat that you will fill it and there will be no room for us. We will tow you across.'

Moon got in gingerly and sat in the bottom of the canoe. The girls jumped into the water, caught the sides of the canoe in their hands, and swam beside it, pulling it across the river. Moon looked over the side and saw their hair streaming in the water and the moonlight dancing on their slim backs. He had never seen the female form so close before. Putting his arms over the side he began to stroke and tickle them. They warned him that if he did not stop they would scream for help.

'Scream as much as you like,' said Bahloo rudely. 'No one will hear you. We are too far away from your camp.'

One of the girls dived under the canoe and joined her friend on the other side.

'Now!' she said.

They put all their weight on the side of the canoe. It tipped over, and with a despairing shriek Bahloo sank into the water. Deeper and deeper down he went, his light dwindling until nothing was to be seen except a silver sliver at the bottom of the water.

The girls hurried home and told what had happened. Some of the older people were glad because Moon would no longer be able to annoy the young women; but others were alarmed at the thought of the dark nights that would follow.

'Moon was good to us,' they said. 'Without him, every night will be dark and dangerous. No one will dare to walk beyond the circle of firelight.'

In their perplexity they asked Wahn the Crow for his advice.

'Perhaps it is a good thing,' he told them. 'Perhaps it is a bad thing. But the nights will be different from now on. I will tell you what will happen. Bahloo is not dead. You can still see a tiny piece of him, and it is shining brightly.'

They peered down into the river.

'Not there,' Wahn said impatiently. 'That is only his reflection. Look up in the sky.'

Sure enough, a thin slice of light was to be seen. It was so thin and pale that it left no shadows on the ground.

'He will get bigger again,' Wahn went on. 'Now he is ashamed, but after a while he will grow more confident. In the end he will be as round as he was before, and again he will try to attract the girls. If they take no notice of him he will grow sad and become small once more. And this will happen now, and for ever and ever more.'

And Wahn was right.

The Husband and Wives who Became Stars

The widow's body was streaked with bands of red and white where the blood had trickled over the lines of mourning pipeclay. She continued to gash herself with a flint knife as she wailed her grief by her husband's grave.

'Why have you taken my husband?' she cried to Nepelle, the ruler of the heavens. 'Why have you not given me a son to comfort me in my sorrow?'

Nepelle heard her cry of anguish.

'Go to the woman quickly,' he said to his servant Nurunderi. 'Take this child with you and give it to her. Her love will find fulfilment in him, and her grief will be assuaged.'

Nurunderi took the child spirit in his arms and descended to earth. He placed the boy under a bush and hid in the scrub to see what would happen. Presently, as the widow lay on the ground exhausted with sobbing, she heard the cry of a baby. Raising herself on her hands, she looked round until she saw a small form in the shadow cast by the bush. She hurried over to it. When she saw that it was a real baby, left ownerless in the desert, she gathered him to her breast and soothed him, until he laughed and put his tiny hand up to her face.

Some inner voice told her that the child should be called Wyungara meaning 'He who returns to the stars'. The boy grew to adolescence, tended by his foster-mother, and fulfilled all her desires for him. He was tall and straight, learned in all the lore she had taught him. In due course he went through the initiation ceremonies of manhood with credit to himself and to her.

Wyungara was hunting one day when he heard the cry of an emu. He crept stealthily through the scrub with his spear held lightly in his hand, ready for instant use, and came to an open space. No emu was there, but a beautiful girl looked steadily at him and then turned her head slowly away.

'Who are you?' he asked.

'My name is Mar-rallang. You are Wyungara. I have heard of you.'

The young man put down his spear and went up to her. They asked questions of each other. They spoke of many things until the sun sank low in the sky and it was time for the girl to go home.

The following day Wyungara went in the same direction and heard, from a nearby marsh, the mating call of a swan. He had been hoping to meet the girl again, but the hunter's instinct was too strong for him. He parted the reeds gently and saw, standing in the water, not a swan, but another young woman.

'What is your name?' he asked.

'I am Mar-rallang.'

He looked at her in surprise.

'Yesterday morning I saw a beautiful girl. Her name was Mar-rallang.'

'I know. She is my sister. We are so much alike that we are both called Two-in-one.'

While talking to the younger Mar-rallang, Wyungara found that the hours passed as swiftly as on the previous day. In the weeks that followed Wyungara spent many hours with the two charming sisters. When he was with one he forgot the other. They were so alike in disposition, so appealing and gentle, that he realised that he was in love with them both. There was only one solution to his problem. He asked them both to become his wife.

His foster-mother's brother raised many objections to the marriage, but Wyungara was insistent. When he saw that his uncle would never consent, he took the two Mar-rallang girls away to a distant part of the country. The three lived happily together. The young husband was so skilful at hunting, and the girls so industrious at finding roots and grubs, that they were well fed and lived together in harmony, content to share each other's love.

Nepelle called Nurunderi to him.

'Why has Wyungara married the daughters of earth?' he enquired. 'Does he not know that the spirits of heaven may not be joined with the daughters of men?'

'No one has told him,' Nurunderi replied. 'He was only a baby when I left him at your command to comfort the widow.'

'They must be separated at once.'

'How can that be done? Shall I bear his spirit back to you and leave the women desolate?'

'No; you will separate them by fire.'

Nurunderi returned to earth. He found the encampment of the lovers and set fire to the dry bushes there. They sprang into crackling life. The flames leapt from one bush to another, and from tree to tree, until the camp was ringed with fire.

Wyungara was asleep, but as the smoke drifted over the shelter fence he woke and sprang to his feet. Through the curtain of smoke he could see the red and yellow flame blossoms. He picked up his spears, caught one of his wives under each arm, and burst through the ring of fire. Then, with his heavy burden, he plunged into a lagoon. The reeds by the bank were dry and caught fire, forcing him to wade further and further into the water, and to submerge himself and his wives from time to time.

The rushes in the middle of the shallow lagoon were green, but they withered in the heat and caught alight. The whole surface of the marsh became one dancing carpet of flame, and the smoke lay as thick and heavy on the water as a kangaroo-skin rug.

'There is no hope for us here,' Wyungara gasped, 'but I will save you.'

He thrust the butt of his longest spear firmly into the mud.

'Great ruler of the sky,' he called, 'save these women. They have done no wrong. Take their hands and lead them to safety.'

The flames licked his body and singed his hair, but he held his spear firmly in one hand and helped them to climb the shaft with the other.

'Hold fast!' he shouted. Then, putting forth all his strength he hurled the spear up into the air. It sped as quickly as a meteor in the night sky. It seemed like a star that had mistaken its direction and was fleeing from earth. It dwindled into the distance and was lost to sight.

Wyungara sank back into the water, content to face death now that his wives were safe. But the heart of Nepelle had been softened by the flame of love that was stronger than the searing heat of the marsh rushes.

The spirit of Wyungara was lifted gently from the lagoon and placed in the sky beside the wives he had loved more than his own life. Nepelle has granted them eternal life and love together in his heavenly home, where they shine steadily—three stars, united for ever.

 ## Nurunderi, the two Girls, and the Evil One

Nepelle, the ruler of the heavens and the father of all spirits, had sent Nurunderi to be his messenger to men and women, to teach them the wisdom that would make them fit to be his children. Nurunderi travelled through every part of the continent until he came to South Australia, where he made his home between Lakes Albert and Alexandrina. Many of the tribesmen were afraid of him. Some ran away and hid in the scrub. When they refused to come out he knew they were not fit to receive the Father Spirit's commands, so he changed them into birds. Those who ventured out and listened to him became skilled in hunting and bushcraft, and wise in all the secrets of nature.

Of all men the Narrinyeri tribe were the most attentive and therefore the most learned. (At least, that is what the Narrinyeri people say.) Nurunderi was so pleased at his reception that he shifted his camp into their territory and waited until Nepelle was ready to tell him that his work was over. From his permanent camp he was able to make excursions to the lakes whenever he required a supply of fish.

On one such expedition he was passing two grass trees standing close together when he heard a doleful cry. Wise as he was, Nurunderi did not know that the voices were those of two sisters who had caused a great deal of trouble to the souls of men as they made their last long journey to the land of spirits. Plants and trees, which were the friends of mankind, had tried to capture the sisters and put an end to them, but they had all failed until one day the grass trees on the banks of Lake Albert had caught them while they were asleep, and imprisoned them. Day after day the girls called to men to release them, but in vain.

They were aware of Nurunderi's presence and were filled with excitement. If only they could persuade Nepelle's own messenger to rescue them!

Nurunderi, whose whole life was devoted to helping others, could not resist their pleas.

'Where are you?' he asked. 'I hear your voices but I cannot see you.'

'We are imprisoned in the grass trees you are looking at. An evil spirit has confined us here. We cannot free ourselves and live the normal life of women until a great and good man such as you comes and rescues us.'

Now at this time Nurunderi was old and tired. His long task ended, he was waiting for the Great Spirit to take him to his eternal home. He had never touched a woman, and had spoken to them only when he had words of advice to give them. He reflected for a while. The element of human nature which guides and often misdirects the wisest of men prompted him to reflect on the joy of companionship that he had missed during his long life. An overwhelming desire to see these women, whose voices came so sweetly and plaintively from the grass trees, swept over him. It was easy to persuade himself that it would be a good deed to release them, even though he realised in his innermost being that there must have been some good reason for their imprisonment.

He made up his mind.

'By the power that is invested in me by the Great Spirit himself I tell you to come out and show yourselves as women.'

The words had hardly been spoken when the two young women stood in front of him. Their eyes were fixed demurely on the ground to hide a mischievous sparkle.

'We are grateful for your help,' they said. 'Our only thought now is to help you, to cook your food, to find roots and grubs to make your meals more tasty when you return from hunting.'

Nurunderi was pleased with their reply.

'Come with me,' he said.

They followed him back to his wurley, giggling when he was out of hearing, and looking sideways at each other. That evening the old man enjoyed his meal as never before. When the moon rose, Nurunderi raised himself on his elbow and looked at the women who lay on either side of him. Unusual feelings of love and protection rose in him. Contentment filled him with a sense of well-being, as though he had found something he had been seeking all his life and had never discovered until that moment.

Weeks passed by in this idyllic manner. There was no work for him to do except fishing and hunting, no message to give to his people. The only thing that troubled him was the occasional thought that Nepelle might soon take him away from his camp and his women. Such forebodings came only when he was alone. During the evening the little glade where the camp was located rang with laughter. At night there was company and the touch of his hand on warm, living flesh.

Nurunderi became so fond of the girls, who had now become his wives, that he could not bear to leave them behind, even when he went across to the lake to fish.

'You can help me there as well as in camp,' he told them. 'Take the small hand-net and try to catch the fish close to the bank.'

He waded out to his waist to catch the larger fish with his spear, while his wives hauled the small net through the shallows.

'See what we have caught!' one whispered excitedly to the other. 'Three tukkeri!'

'But they are only for men. We are not allowed to eat them.'

'Why shouldn't we? The old man will never know. I don't see why men should always keep the best food for themselves.'

'All right. Let's put them in our bags and cover them with rushes so the old man won't see them.'

They called to their husband, 'We are going back to camp now. There are no fish here. We'll dig some yams and have the fire ready for you when you bring your catch home.'

He waved his spear to show them he had heard, and went on with his fishing. The young women ran back to the camp, built up the fire, and baked the fish they had caught.

'No wonder the men keep it to themselves,' the wives said as they sank their teeth into the succulent white flesh. 'This is better than wallaby meat or the big, coarse fish old Messenger catches for us. We'll go back another time and get some more.'

The gentle breeze carried the smell of the cooked fish down the slope of the hill and across the water. Nurunderi straightened himself and sniffed suspiciously.

'Tukkeri! Surely my wives are not cooking the forbidden fish?'

He waded ashore hurriedly and ran towards the camp. When he arrived he found the fire burning. Everywhere there was a strong smell of cooked fish and tukkeri oil, but of his wives there was no sign. They had seen him coming and had gone down to the edge of the lake by another path. They pulled an old raft from its hiding place in the reeds and paddled towards the far side of the lake.

Nurunderi was aghast. For the first time he realised that young women do not mate readily with an old man, and that he had been deceived by them. Shading his eyes, he looked across the lake and saw the black dot in the middle of the water. It was all that could be seen of the raft and the runaway wives. Pausing only to make sure that he had all his weapons, the old man ran to his canoe and set out in pursuit.

It was dark when he reached the far side, but he could see where the women had landed, and was satisfied that he could follow their trail in the morning. He lit a fire, cooked food, and examined his weapons again before going to sleep. Among them was a plongge, a short weapon with a knob at one end, used to inflict bruises on anyone who broke the tribal laws. He fingered it with a grim smile on his face, and lay down to sleep with the weapon cradled in his arm.

All the next morning he followed the two sets of footprints, but lost the trail when it came to stony ground. He made several casts, trying to cut the track where it was likely to come out on soft ground, but though he searched throughout the afternoon, he could not find it again.

Dispirited and lonely, he made his camp fire in the late afternoon and prepared for the night. While he was half awake, half asleep, Puckowie the Grandmother Spirit came to him, and warned him that danger was near. In the early morning he was fully on guard, but he could see no sign of an enemy. The only living thing in sight was a wombat. Learned man that he was, still he did not recognise that the Evil One himself had taken this shape to deceive him.

Nurunderi was hungry. He stalked the wombat and killed it. When he drew his spear from its body, blood poured on to the sand. He carried the animal back to his overnight camp and was making up the fire ready to roast the flesh, when he remembered that he had left his spear behind. He hurried back and saw a strange sight. The wombat's blood had congealed and was stirring in the sand. Nurunderi watched it gather itself up until it took the form of a man lying prone on the ground. After a long time the face and features were fully formed. The man was alive, but appeared to be sleeping.

'Perhaps he will be a friend to me, and will help me in my search for those wicked women,' thought Nurunderi.

He left his spear behind as a gift and went into the bush to make another for his own use. When he returned the man and the spear had gone. Nurunderi could see the shallow depression where the body had been lying, but there was no sign of any footprints leading away from it. He sat down to consider the matter. Friends always leave footprints. It is only an enemy who destroys his trail, but in this case Nurunderi could think of no way in which it could have been disguised. He was worried. The recollection of Puckowie's warning came back to him, and he kept a careful watch.

Before long he heard a sound which came from the further side of a large sandhill. He sidled round it and saw the figure of the Evil One, who had now resumed his normal appearance.

'Are you the man who came from the blood of the wombat this morning?' asked Nurunderi.

'It may be that I am; it may be that I am not.'

Nurunderi looked at him more closely.

'You are that man,' he said. 'That is my spear you are holding.'

'Then you may have it back,' the Evil One replied, and swung it backwards, ready to hurl it at Nurunderi.

'Wait!' the Messenger cried. 'I gave you that spear in case you should need it. It was an act of friendship. I want you to help me.'

The Evil One laughed sardonically.

'What help do you think I can give you?'

'I am looking for my wives. They did an evil deed and then ran away. I want to find them.'

'Why?'

'So that I can give them the punishment they deserve.'

The Evil One laughed again.

'Then you will get no help from me, Nurunderi. I know who you are. You are the teacher Nepelle sent into the world to help men. You are old and you have offended against his law. You are at my mercy. I am the Evil One.'

Nurunderi's heart sank. He regretted his weakness in marrying the young women. He realised that he had put himself at the mercy of the enemy of Nepelle. He tried to divert the other's attention.

'You can't be the Evil One. He would never enter into the body of a wombat!'

'I can take any form I want,' the Evil One retorted. 'But in this case I admit that I was a prisoner of the wombat. I tried to attack you many times, but the good spirits prevented me, and shut me up in the body of a wombat. Then you forgot Nepelle's teaching and fell under the spell of two foolish girls. They deceived you. When they fled it was I who made them come this way. You killed the wombat and released me from my prison.'

'Then you should regard me as your friend.'

'No, you are not my friend. And you have forfeited the friendship of Nepelle. You are just a lonely old man who is about to die at the hand of the Evil One!'

He hurled the spear at Nurunderi like a bolt of lightning. The teacher leapt aside, but not quickly enough. The spear pierced his leg. He stooped and drew it out.

'Now you are at my mercy,' Nurunderi cried in triumph. He threw the spear back with all his might, straight into the heart of the Evil One.

The old man cried aloud in gratitude to Nepelle, thinking that the Father Spirit had forgiven him, and prepared to resume his journey. He walked for several hours, until it dawned slowly on him that he was making no progress. His heart sank again. He recognised the same sandhills, the same trees and, when he turned and looked back, the same body of the Evil One lying on the ground. He crouched down and watched it closely. He saw that birds, small animals, and insects which approached the body were unable to escape.

'The spirit of the Evil One is still alive,' he thought, 'even though I have killed his outward form. I must destroy the body completely and all will be well.'

He gathered scrub and dry sticks and built a huge funeral pyre. He dragged the body on to it and waited until it was consumed by the flames. Then he turned to leave the haunted place. But still he found himself unable to escape. A careful examination of the ground showed that the blood of the man had soaked into the sand. Nurunderi raked the embers across so that the blood was burned, and at last he found he was free to depart. The animals and insects, suddenly released, danced round him trying to express their gratitude.

Many leagues lay behind him when he came to the bank of the Murray River. Two sets of footprints showed that his wives had come this way. The tracks stopped at the water's edge, and he knew that they must have crossed by means of a canoe or raft. There was no way for Nurunderi to cross. He prayed to Nepelle, and to his relief the earth trembled, heaped itself up, and a long tongue of sand and rock stretched out across the river, forming a bridge which he crossed at a run.

'It is a sign of forgiveness!' he said.

The next day he reached the sea. The ashes of a camp fire lay on the sand. Shells and the remains of a meal showed that the young women were still eating forbidden food. Nurunderi sat down on the sand and wept. His tears flowed together and ran in rivulets, soaking into the ground and forming a pool which overflowed and trickled into the sea. The pool remains in that place, but because of the love of Nepelle for his erring teacher, the water is no longer salt. It has become clear and fresh, and sustains the spirits of the departed who are seeking the land of eternal life.

The following morning, as soon as it was light, Nurunderi saw a peninsula at a little distance from the shore. It was connected by a long, narrow strip to the land, but it was evident that at flood tide the higher ground at the end would be cut off from the shore by the water. The keeper of the isthmus was Ga-ra-gah the Blue Crane, who guarded the approach. The young women sat close to the shore, talking to the Crane.

Far away though they were, Nurunderi realised that they were using their powers of persuasion to induce the keeper to let them cross. Nurunderi shouted and saw them turn and look at him. He beckoned, but they turned and spoked even more earnestly to Ga-ra-gah. One of them put her arms round his neck. Blue Crane stepped to one side and they began to run along the causeway.

'This is your opportunity!'

It was faithful old Puckowie whispering in his ear.

'Help me, Nepelle,' cried Nurunderi. 'In your wisdom you know what should be done to the wives whom I have loved so well and so foolishly. They are young. Remember this, and forgive me for my wrong-doing which has been so much greater than theirs.'

'They are entering the Spirit Land,' Puckowie whispered again. 'It is the will of Nepelle that you should chant the wind song. Quickly!'

Nurunderi threw back his head and began to sing. A puff of wind caught the words and blew them towards the peninsula. The waves leaped to hear them. The wind caught their crests and blew them to a fine spray which drenched the racing girls. The sea lifted itself from its bed, surged over the land, and swept the young women from their feet. The wind howled across the sea until the waves broke over their heads and they were lost to sight. The tears ran in streams down Nurunderi's cheeks as he sat watching and grieving for them.

The wind died away quickly. The sun shone out on a calm sea between the shore and the little island which had now become the Island of the Spirit Land. At a short distance two rounded rocks rose above the water.

'They are your wives,' Puckowie said. 'Nepelle has turned them to stone, and will not allow them to go to the Spirit Land.'

The tears dropped from the old man's chin.

'They do not deserve that,' he whispered brokenly. 'They were so young, so beautiful. They did not understand what they were doing. Nepelle is all-forgiving. He will not let his servant suffer.'

He threw himself into the water. His body was seized in the grip of current which swept him down to the bottom of the ocean, where he met the spirits of his young wives. All three clung together, and felt themselves lifted up through the water, into the clear air, up through thick folds of clouds until they reached the very heavesns, where Nepelle lets them shine as stars to show that he has forgiven them.

It was because Nurunderi loved his wives so greatly that they were forgiven and allowed to live together in the starry sky; but their petrified bodies remain in the sea as a warning to all women never to eat forbidden food.

 Eagle-hawk and the Woodpeckers

The yaraan tree soared up into the sky. It was as tall as five trees.* The topmost branches were so far away that they could hardly be seen, and indeed there were times when they were hidden from sight by low-lying clouds. It was here that Mullian the Eagle-hawk lived with his wife Moodai the Possum, his mother-in-law Moodai, who was also a Possum, and Butterga the Flying Squirrel.

One man and three women, and every one of them a cannibal! Mullian was taller and stronger and braver than his women. When they cried, 'Mullian, we are hungry!' the mighty Eagle-hawk would climb down from his home, armed with a spear which was too heavy for any other man to carry. He would follow the trail of any two-legged man until he caught up with him.

Thud! Mullian's spear would crash into his body, and that was the end of the unfortunate man. Leaving the lifeless body impaled on his spear, Mullian would throw it over his shoulder, walk back to the yaraan tree and

---

* One version of the legend states that the tall tree, which grew by the Barwon River, was actually composed of five different trees—gum, boxtree, coolabah, belar, and pine. The progress of those who climbed the tree could be followed by the chips of bark which fell down.

run swiftly up the smooth trunk with the grisly meal dangling at the end of his spear.

When he reached the little humpy on the branches far away in the clouds, the fire would be burning brightly. The women would dismember the body and cook it on the hot stones.

For a long time no one knew that Mullian was killing the men who lived on the ground, but one day he was seen running swiftly with the body of a young woman transfixed by his spear.

'What shall we do?' the men asked each other. 'It is not right that Mullian should be allowed to kill men and women.'

'Wait till he comes down and we'll ambush him,' someone suggested; but there were plenty of men to advise against such a foolhardy idea.

'Twenty men could not overcome Mullian,' they said. 'They would die, and nothing would be achieved but an extra large meal for his women-folk.'

'Then someone had better climb up the yaraan tree and set fire to his humpy.'

A little old man who was noted for his prowess as a hunter burst into a cackling laugh.

'Oh yes, climb up the tree and set fire to his humpy,' he mocked. 'Put wings on your feet and soar like a bird. Or cover them with gum and walk up the trunk like a fly.'

'The Bibbis can do it,' called a voice out of the darkness.

Two strong, active young Bibbis who belonged to the Woodpecker tribe jumped into the firelight.

'Ho ho! We are the men to do it,' they shouted, and they danced round the fire. Their arms and legs jerked up and down as though they were climbing the tree.

'That's how we will climb the tree.'

The old man laughed again.

'Very good, you Bibbis, but how will you set fire to the humpy?'

'Like this,' said a squeaky voice from above them. Murra-wunda the Climbing Rat sprang out of an overhanging branch and landed inside the circle of men. As he flew through the air he left a trail of smoke and flame behind him. When he stood up they saw that he was holding a lighted twig between his teeth. He had stolen it from the fire while everyone was looking at the old hunter.

'Good, Murra-wunda, good. You may come with us,' the Bibbi men said approvingly.

Early next morning the three eager young men began to climb the trunk of the yaraan tree. They were frightened when the tree shook, because Mullian was descending on one of his hunting trips, but they hid on the other side of the trunk and he did not see them. All day they climbed. When night fell they were less than halfway up. They camped for the night on a broad branch, fearful lest Mullian should discover them on his way home; but Eagle-hawk must have had to forage far afield for food, for he did not pass them during the hours of darkness.

The following morning they reached the platform where Mullian had built his home. The women were busy preparing vegetable food as relish for the meal they expected Mullian to bring them. Murra-wunda and the Bibbis crept into the humpy unseen. Climbing Rat had nursed the smouldering twig carefully. He tucked it into a dark corner where it would keep on smouldering until the red ember touched the grass wall.

'Now we shall see the sight of a lifetime,' Murra-wunda whispered. 'Come on. If we don't get down quickly we'll be in trouble.'

They slid over the edge of the platform and climbed down the trunk much more quickly than they had gone up. Safe on the ground once more they waited until Mullian had gone past. In spite of his load he swung himself up effortlessly from branch to branch, and dwindled in size until he seemed as small as an insect. The tiny black dot reached the aerial home and disappeared from sight.

The climbers called to their friends to come and watch. Soon the tree was surrounded with a circle of upturned faces. Unaware of the expectant gaze of the men below, Mullian tossed the body he had brought to Butterga and the two Moodias and went into the grass shelter.

'Something is burning,' he called.

'It's only the cooking fire,' Butterga said.

Mullian was not satisfied.

'The humpy is full of smoke,' he said. 'Come and see if you can find out what's wrong.'

The women crowded inside and began to cough. The smoke grew thicker and they could hardly see each other. A red glow sprang to life in the far corner, and with a roar the whole wall burst into flames. The women fled to the opening in the far wall, but Mullian was ahead of them. The hut creaked and sagged a little. His broad shoulders were caught in the doorway.

Now the flames licked against the roof, which flowered into a blaze of yellow flame. To the watchers far below it seemed as though the yaraan tree had put forth a beautiful flower, but for Mullian and his wives it was the flower of death.

Mullian's arm was burnt off at the shoulder. With singed hair and bursting skin the women fell unconscious to the floor. The flames roared as they consumed the bodies. Soon nothing was left on the bare branch but the charred bones of the four cannibals.

Strong in death as he had been in life, the spirit of Mullian soared away from the yaraan tree taking the soul of one wife with him. Moodai the mother-in-law and Butterga the Flying Squirrel were left behind, but up in the sky Mullian took his place as Mullian-ga, the Morning Star. By his side is a faint star which is his arm, separated from his body, and a larger one which is Moodai his wife.

The fire burnt down the trunk of the yaraan tree and along the roots until nothing was left. The earth fell in when the roots were consumed, leaving channels along which water flows, in time of flood, into the great hole where the barrel of the tree once grew from the ground.

The Seven Sisters

It was in the Dreamtime that girls decided that they should go through severe tests to show that they were ready for womanhood and marriage, just as the young men had to prove themselves for manhood. They went to the elders of the tribe and told them what they had decided. The leading men and the old ones sat late that night nodding their heads and speaking slowly. In the morning they summoned the girls to the council. They told them that they approved their decision and commended them for their wisdom.

'But what is it you want to do?' they asked.

'We want to show that our minds are not ruled by our bodies. We believe that women, as well as men, should be able to overcome fear and pain. Then our sons will be brave and strong in the years to come. Give us the same sort of tests as the boys,' they pleaded.

The wise men looked at each other questioningly. Only grown men were allowed to know what boys had to endure during the initiation tests.

'We shall make new tests,' they said after they had thought about it for a long time. 'Girls could never stand the ordeals that boys have to go through.'

The young women stood firm.

'In days to come we will give birth to boys who will be subject to the rites. It is only fitting that we, who will be their mothers, should know what they will have to go through when they are older. They will be bone of our bone, flesh of our flesh. If we conquer fear and pain, they will be strong when their time comes.'

'Very well,' the elders said. 'We would never willingly have made you suffer; but if you can endure to the end you will win our respect, and we shall think the more of our women.'

It was no light thing that the girls had undertaken. For three years they were taken to a place where no one else was allowed to go. The elders taught them the law of the tribe. They gave them only a small portion of food at sunrise and another at sunset. Their bodies became lean and sinewy, until they felt that they had learned to control their appetites.

'Now we are ready,' they said.

'No,' the elders replied. 'For three years you have endured your training. Now the time for the testing has come. The first test will show whether you have learned the first lesson.'

They were taken on a long, difficult journey for three days. They went through dense bush where thorns and sharp stakes scratched and tore their flesh; they crossed burning plains and high mountains, and in all that time they were not permitted to touch food. On the morning of the fourth day the elders caught kangaroos and wallabies, and gave each girl a flint knife.

'Cut your food with this,' they said. 'Take as much as you want to satisfy your appetites.'

To the relief of the elders the young women took only enough meat to satisfy their immediate hunger. If they had obeyed their instincts they would have taken the whole joint to distend their stomachs after the long fast, but they had learnt the lesson well.

They returned to camp and the second series of tests began.

'This is to see whether you have overcome pain,' they were warned.

One by one they were made to lie flat on their backs on the bare ground. A wirinun took a pointed stick, thrust it between a girl's lips so that it rested on a front tooth, and hit the butt of the stick with repeated blows until the tooth was knocked out.

'Are you ready to lose another tooth?' she was asked.

'Yes.'

A second tooth was knocked out, but the girl made no sound. The others submitted themselves to the ordeal without protest.

'Now stand in a row,' the wirinun commanded. With a sharp flint he scored heavy lines across their breasts until the blood flowed down their stomachs and dropped on to the ground. Ashes were rubbed into the wounds to increase the pain, but they endured the double agony without a murmur.

'Now you may lie down and go to sleep,' they were told.

They stretched out on the bare ground and sank into a sleep of exhaustion, forgetting for a little while their aching gums and the wounds in which ashes stung as they healed the jagged cuts. Several hours later one of the girls woke and smothered a scream before it reached her lips. She felt something moving across her body. She tensed her muscles until they were as hard as wood. Every part of her was covered with crawling insects. They slithered across her lips, wormed their way into her nostrils and ears, and over her eyelids, but she remained silent and motionless; and so with every girl, until daylight came to release them.

The tests continued until it seemed that there was no end to them: there was the ordeal of the pierced nose, in which they were required to wear a stick, which kept the wound from healing, through the septum. Every time it was touched it was agony to the wearer as it tore further through the flesh. There was the ordeal of the bed of hot cinders; and others that degraded the body and could be overcome only by steadfastness of mind and spirit.

'It is over,' the elders said at last. 'You have endured every ordeal, every test of pain, every torture, with fortitude and cheerfulness. The elders of your tribe are proud of you. There now remains the last test, the conquering of fear. You have gone a long way towards it. Do you think you can survive this as well?'

'We can!' cried the girls with a single voice.

The ordeal came at night. The old men went to the isolated camp where the girls were to sleep without the comfort of fire, where the wind moaned eerily in the trees, and the spirits of darkness and evil seemed to hide in every bush. The elders chanted spine-chilling tales of bunyips and maldarpes, of the Yara-ma-yha-who and the Keen Keeng, of monsters such as the Whowhie, Thardid Jimbo, and Cheeroonear, and of the Evil One himself. Then they stole away, and the girls were left all alone.

Horrible screams came from the surrounding bush and continued all night, as though the encampment was surrounded by spirits and monsters. The old men enjoyed themselves as they endeavoured to fill the girls' hearts with fear; but the young women who had passed through pain to the ultimate test of womanhood were able to call on their hard-won reserves of courage and endurance.

Morning came. The whole tribe came out to greet them and congratulate them on the triumph of mind over body. On that day even the gods and spirits of the high heaven were present. The girls, now entered into full womanhood, were snatched from the midst of their friends and taken up to the sky where, as the Seven Sisters of the constellation of the Pleiades, they shine down serenely on the world, encouraging every successive generation to follow their example.

But there is another tribal tale which gives the names of the Seven Sisters as Meamei. They were the custodians of a unique treasure, the gift of fire, which they kept hidden in their yam sticks. They cooked their food with it and lit the fires that warmed them at night. When the weather was cold, men and women came to them and begged for the fire; but the hearts of the Meamei were as hard as mountain rocks.

'This is our possession,' they boasted. 'We will not share it with anyone.'

Amongst those who had been repulsed by the sisters was Wahn the Crow. Others had gone away disappointed, but it was not in Wahn's nature to accept a rebuff. He knew there must be some way of getting the fire away from the Meamei, so he hid in a tree and watched everything they did. Soon he discovered that they were fond of eating white ants. They spent a great deal of their time searching for them, and when they had gathered a quantity, they ate them for their evening meal.

Wahn went off to a little distance and caught a number of poisonous snakes, which he sealed inside a termite nest. He hurried back to the Meamei and said excitedly, 'I have found an enormous termite hill. Come with me. I'll show you where it is.'

The Seven Sisters followed him, licking their lips in anticipation. When they reached the ant hill they broke it down with their yam sticks. To their dismay a number of hissing snakes glided out and darted at them. The sisters struck wildly at them with their yam sticks, till the ends of the sticks broke off and the fire fell on the ground. Wahn crept into their midst, picked up the fire, and carried it away.

It was after this that the Seven Sisters went up into the sky and became the constellation of the Pleiades. The gift of fire was now in the possession of Crow, who guarded it as jealously as its previous owners. Mankind had expected that he would make it available to everyone, but Wahn had a much more cunning plan.

'I am now the custodian of fire,' he told them. 'It is a sacred trust conferred on me by Baiame—as a reward for my own courage and cleverness,' he added hastily. 'I am not permitted to share it with you, but I am anxious to help you. If you bring your food to me, I will cook it for you.'

The people applauded his generosity, and Wahn kept his promise. He cooked their food when it was brought to him, but he always kept the choicest pieces for himself.

'Why don't you hunt for your own food?' they asked him.

Wahn reproached them.

'You are ungrateful,' he said. 'I cook your food for you. The least you can do is to supply my modest requirements. The custodian of fire has no time to go looking for food.'

The people complained to Baiame. The Great Spirit was angry when he heard what Wahn was doing. He told the people not to be afraid, but to take the fire away from Wahn by force.

So they gathered together and rushed Crow's camp. As they drew close he threw the burning logs at them to drive off the attackers, who snatched them up and carried them away to start their own camp fires. Wahn was left alone. He chuckled to himself when he thought how easily he had escaped; but he had forgotten that the all-seeing Father Spirit could see everything that happened in the world he had created.

Baiame cursed the Crow.

'May you be as black as the charred wood of your fire,' he thundered. 'You do not deserve to be a man.'

He pointed at Wahn, whose body began to shrink. His legs became like little sticks, his face elongated, terminating in a beak, and feathers sprouted from his arms. There he stood: no longer Wahn the man, but Wahn the Crow—black as the burnt logs that fall from the fire.

Before the Meamei sisters left the earth they went into the mountains and made springs of water to feed the rivers, so that there would be water for men and women for all time. A young hunter Karambal was sorrowful when he heard the Meamei sisters were leaving because he had fallen in love with one of them. When he found the girl alone one day he carried her off to be his wife. But the other sisters sent cold wintry weather to the earth to force the hunter to release their sister. After this they made their departure into the sky in search of summer, to melt the snow and ice.

It is at summer time every year that they appear, bringing the hot days with them. After the hot weather they travel far to the west, and winter comes to remind men that it is wrong to carry off women who belong to a totem that is forbidden them.

After his experience with the Meamei, Karambal went in search of another wife. He thought he had learnt his lesson, and was determined to choose one of the right totem. When he found the woman he wanted he was again unfortunate, for she was already married to a great warrior whose name was Bullabogabun. With soft words Karambal induced the woman to leave her husband and go away with him.

Their life together was short and sweet. Bullabogabun followed their tracks and speedily overtook them. Karambal's love was less than his fear. Abandoning the woman, he climbed a tall tree which grew near the camp and hid in the branches. Bullabogabun saw him crouched there, and lit a fire at the base of the tree. The branches caught fire, and then the trunk, which blazed like the torch of a giant in the midst of the plain. Karambal was borne up by the hungry flames and rode on them into the sky, close to the Seven Sisters. Forgetting all that he had learned, he still pursues them through the sky—Karambal, who became the star Aldebaran, the pursuer.

 ## The Brush Turkeys of the Sky

In the Dreamtime there was a large plain where no one lived except a flock of brush turkeys. They were free to roam wherever they wanted, and they had no enemies. Life would have been very pleasant if it had not been for Old Grandfather Brush Turkey, who was still strong and vigorous, and larger than all the other birds. He had never been popular with the rest of the flock, and had withdrawn into himself, often absenting himself for long periods.

There was an outcry when it was discovered that one of the younger birds was missing.

'Where can she have gone?' everyone asked. 'We saw her at the dance last night, but now there is no sign of her.'

One of the birds plucked up courage and went to look for Grandfather Brush Turkey.

'Have you seen our little one?' he asked.

'How should I know?' the old bird answered gruffly. 'None of you take any notice of me. Why should I notice you?'

The young bird went away sorely puzzled, for he had seen feathers and a trickle of dried blood on the ground, but had not dared to ask more questions.

The matter was forgotten for several days, and then another bird went missing. The hunters examined the ground cautiously. They saw signs of a body which had been dragged through the bushes, more feathers, and a pathetic heap of bones.

'It is old Grandfather Turkey,' they told the rest of the flock that night. 'He has become a cannibal. He waits until we dance in the moonlight. Then he pounces on one of the younger birds when it is overcome with fatigue, and drags it away and kills it.'

'What shall we do? We cannot permit the old Grandfather to do this to our loved ones.'

'What can we do?'

'We can go and kill him.'

'Who dares to go?'

There was a long silence. It was obvious that something should be done to remove the danger, but no one dared to attack the oldest and biggest and strongest of the Brush Turkeys.

In the absence of any bird with sufficient courage to rid them of the peril, they had to endure the loss of the young birds.

'It would be easy to forego our dances,' a mother bird said one day. 'It is only when the youngsters become tired during the dance and fall over that Grandfather is able to carry them away and kill them.'

They all agreed with her, but the next night they were dancing again under the bright moon. The moonlight was in their blood, and if they stopped dancing they would no longer be brush turkeys.

But this state of affairs could not go on indefinitely, or the whole flock would diminish and be lost in the silence of the desert.

Another conference was called.

'There is only one thing left to us,' said one of the leaders. 'We cannot fight; nor can we stay here waiting to be killed. We must go away to some place where Grandfather cannot find us.'

'When shall we go?' came a chorus of voices, because everyone agreed with him.

'We shall go now,' he said unexpectedly. 'We could think about it for a long time and talk about it; perhaps old Grandfather would overhear us, and he would follow. Last night he stole one of our finest girls, and now he will be lying asleep somewhere so full of food that he will not be able to move.'

A long procession set out. They tried to conceal their tracks so that the cannibal turkey would not be able to follow; but how can a great company of birds go walkabout without leaving traces of their passage?

Two days later, when morning came and his appetite was revived,

Grandfather Brush Turkey realised that the desert was silent. He fluttered into the branches of a tree and looked about. Nowhere could he see the rest of his flock, who should have been browsing on the plain. He hurried to their dancing ground and saw the beaten circle where the dances had been held, and a clear trail that led towards the mountains. Fluttering his wings, he ran along it until he came to the mountains. It was more difficult to follow the trail over the stones, but here and there he found a telltale mark, or a feather that had dropped to the ground. Even when the flock had waded down the bed of a stream he could read the signs in the disturbed leaves and the feathers caught in bushy twigs.

Presently he came to an outcrop of rock where there was a clear view of the plains on the further side of the mountain. Shading the sun from his eyes with one wing, he stared intently until he saw the distant specks which told him where his flock had camped.

The old bird smiled inwardly. He waited till dusk before going near the camp and hiding in some dense bush.

'The mountain air has sharpened my appetite,' he said to himself. 'And these bushes are wonderfully placed to give cover, and yet so handy that I can pounce on to the dancing ring without being seen.'

He settled down to wait. He had no way of telling that when the flock had reached the new encampment, the birds had been visited by two large brush turkeys who had flown down to them from somewhere in Baiame's realm in the sky.

'Why have you come here?' the two birds asked the turkeys of the plain. 'What is the matter with your home over the mountains?'

The brush turkeys gathered round them and all began to talk at once. From the babble of sound the visitors learned of Grandfather Brush Turkey and what he was doing to the flock.

They looked at each other understandingly and said, 'We understand. Baiame tells us that what you have done is right. Do not fear. Tonight you must have your dance as usual. Don't take any notice of anything that may happen.'

Grandfather Brush Turkey remained hidden in the bushes, watching the dancers intently in the soft light of the moon. Behind and a little to one side the two Sky Brush Turkeys were hidden, watching old Grandfather Brush Turkey.

As the night went on the dancers grew more excited; their songs and their dancing feet went quicker and quicker. One of the young birds fell to the ground. Grandfather Turkey sprang to his feet, pushed his way through the brush, and stooped over the body. But at that moment a huge bird towered over him and struck him such a blow that he rolled over on the ground. Grandfather Turkey lay on his back and looked up with an expression of dismay on his old, wrinkled face. Another great bird came from behind, there was a soft sound of a second blow, and the cannibal lay dead on the rim of the dancing floor.

The birds went on dancing, taking no notice of what had happened, until the sky visitors called them.

'That is the end of your troubles,' they said. 'Old Grandfather will never kill your young birds again.'

The whole flock gobbled and clucked with admiration and relief. From their midst the huge birds rose, flapping their wings majestically, and mounted up into the sky. As a reward for their services to the smaller birds of earth, Baiame stretched out his hand and placed them in the sky where, as guides for the spirits of the heavens and for men on earth, they became two specks of light that point to the burning stars of the Southern Cross.

 ## The Dancing of Priepriggie

Like sparks from a burning branch when it is struck on the ground, so the stars flew aimlessly through the dark sky. In a little valley in Queensland men and women danced their nightly dance, led by Priepriggie, the singer of songs, the whirler of bullroarers, the skilled huntsman, the wirinun with the flying feet. They sang his songs and danced his songs, while the stars left fiery trails in the sky, in a confusion of light and bewildering chaos. Above there was no order or rhythm, but in the little valley the chanting and the dancing footsteps blended as Priepriggie's people followed him round the magic circle. Their hearts thumped in the rhythm, and when the singing was over and they sank exhausted to the ground, they murmured to each other, 'Great is Priepriggie. If he wished he could even make the stars dance to his songs!'

Men and women who spend the long hours of the night dancing, and who sleep till dawn, need food to sustain their bodies. The women had their tasks, and the men were hunters; but of all who sought for food, Priepriggie was the most successful. He was first up at dawn, and this morning he stole through the pearly grey mist by the river bank until he came to the huge tree where the flying foxes hung from the branches. They had returned from their nightly flight, and were sound asleep.

His footfall was as light as the glint of sunbeams on the grass, and not a twig stirred, not a drop of dew fell from the leaves as he made his way towards the tree. The flying foxes hung in clusters from the bare branches. There was little food for a man or woman in a flying fox, but their leader was many times the size of his followers, and it was the leader whom Priepriggie was seeking in order to provide his people with a meal that night.

Closer still he moved, until at last he could see the huge body of the leader of the flying foxes, surrounded by his wives and attendants. Priepriggie fitted the butt of his spear into his woomera, and drew it back, inch by inch, until his arm was fully stretched behind him. Then, with one convulsive thrust, with every ounce of body and muscles behind it, the throwing stick swept forward and the spear sang through the air. It pierced the body of the great flying fox and pinned it to the tree trunk. A moment later there was a deafening roar as the flying foxes woke and spread their wings. They flew out of the tree like a cloud of smoke and circled round, waiting for their leader.

He did not come. Presently they saw his body against the trunk, with the shaft of the spear still vibrating. With another circling of the tree they saw Priepriggie crouched on the ground, his woomera in front of him. Like a cloud of flies they descended on him, lifted him up and bore him away. Higher and higher they mounted until they disappeared from sight.

That night men and women searched for the singer of songs, but they could not see him anywhere. Their bellies were empty, because their hunting had not been successful, and a sadness descended on them.

'Without Priepriggie we are helpless,' they cried. 'If we dance this dance, perhaps he will come back to us. Perhaps he is lost, and is waiting to hear our songs.'

They broke into a shuffling dance, but it had no life in it. Suddenly they stopped. They heard the sound of someone singing. It came from a long distance, and seemed to come from the stars.

'Listen! It is the voice of Priepriggie,' they said.

The song grew louder; a compelling rhythm beat through their heads, and set their blood running faster.

'Look! The stars are dancing.'

The random, darting stars had arranged themselves in order, and were dancing to Priepriggie's song. The men and women joined in. Their feet flew over the ground, the song rose from deep in their bodies and burst out of their throats. The new dance of Priepriggie was danced on earth and in the sky.

The song was over. The dance was finished. They lay back and stared in amazement. Right across the sky the stars were resting in a ribbon of light. The dancers of the heavens were lying where they had fallen when the corroboree of the skies ended. Though men mourned the loss of Priepriggie, they rejoiced because the Milky Way was spread above them to remind them that Priepriggie could charm the stars of heaven as easily as the feet of men.

Part III

Legends of Animals

The Last of his Tribe

He crouches, and buries his face on his knees,
    And hides in the dark of his hair;
For he cannot look up to the storm-smitten trees,
    Or think of the loneliness there—
    Or the loss and the loneliness there.

The wallaroos grope through the tufts of the grass,
    And turn to their coverts for fear;
But he sits in the ashes and lets them pass
    Where the boomerangs sleep with the spear—
    With the nullah, the sling and the spear.

Uloola, behold him! the thunder that breaks
    On the tops of the rocks with the rain,
And the wind which drives up with the salt of the lakes,
    Have made him a hunter again—
    A hunter and fisher again.

For his eyes have been full with a smouldering thought;
    But he dreams of the hunts of yore,
And of foes that he sought, and of fights that he fought
    With those who will battle no more—
    Who will go to the battle no more.

It is well that the water which tumbles and fills,
    Goes moaning and moaning along;

For an echo rolls out from the sides of the hills,
   And he starts at a wonderful song—
   At the sound of a wonderful song.

And he sees, through the rents of the scattering fogs,
   The corroboree warlike and grim,
And the lubra who sat by the fire on the logs,
To watch, like a mourner, for him—
   Like a mother and mourner for him.

Will he go in his sleep from these desolate lands,
   Like a chief, to the rest or his race,
With the honey-voiced woman who beckons and stands,
   And gleams like a dream in his face—
   Like a marvellous dream in his face?

Henry Kendall

 ## How the Animals Came to Australia

Long before there were men or animals in Australia,* the only living things
that had eyes to see the vast continent were flocks of migratory birds. When
they returned to their homeland far to the east, they told the animals, which
at that time had the form of men and women, of the unending plains, the
tree-covered mountains, the wide, long rivers, and the abundant vegetation
of the great land over which they had flown. The reports created such

---

* This legend is also related in *Aboriginal Fables and Legendary Tales* by the same author. It
is included in the present compilation because it may be regarded as the basic story of the arrival
of the animals in Australia when they were still men. In this legend and others that follow, we
see how the actions of men led to the characteristic forms of the animals which succeeded them,
in a reversal of the evolutionary system. The first printed version was recorded by R. H. Mathews
in the journal *Science of Man*, and in his book *Folklore of the Australian Aborigines* he referred
to it as the origin of the Thurrawai tribe.

excitement that the animals assembled from far and near to hold a corroboree and discuss the matter. It was decided that, as the land appeared to be so much richer and more desirable than their own, they would all go and live there.

The big problem was how to reach the land of promise. Every animal had its own canoe, but they were frail craft, well suited to the placid waters of lakes and streams, but not to the ocean that lay between the two lands. The only vessel that could contain them all was the one that belonged to Whale. He was asked if he would lend it to them, but he gave a flat refusal.

The animals were determined to migrate, no matter what difficulties had to be overcome. They held another secret meeting at which they enlisted the aid of Starfish, who was Whale's closest friend. Starfish agreed to help, for he was as anxious as the others to make the journey.

'Greetings, my friend,' he said to Whale.

'Greetings,' Whale replied in his deep, rumbling voice. 'What do you want?'

'There is nothing I want, except to help you. I see your hair is badly infested with lice. I thought that as I am so small I could pick them off for you.'

'That's extraordinarily kind of you. They do worry me a bit,' Whale admitted. He placed his head in Starfish's lap and gave a sensuous wriggle of contentment. Starfish plucked off the lice in a leisurely fashion.

While the cleaning task went on, the animals went on tiptoe to the shore, loaded all their possessions in Whale's huge canoe, and paddled silently out to sea. The faint splash of their paddles was drowned by Starfish as he scratched vigorously at the vermin.

After a while Whale became restless, and began to fret.

'Where is my canoe?' he asked. 'I can't see it.'

'It's here, right beside you,' said Starfish soothingly.

He picked up a piece of wood and struck a hollow log by his side. It gave out a booming noise.

'Are you satisfied now?'

Whale sank back again and submitted himself to his friend's attentions once more. The sun was low in the sky when Whale woke up for a second time.

'I am anxious about my canoe,' he said. 'Let me see it.'

He brushed Starfish aside and rolled over so that he could look round him. There was a long furrow in the sand where the canoe had been pulled down the beach, but of the canoe itself there was no sign. Whale turned round in alarm and saw it on the distant horizon, almost lost to sight. He turned on Starfish and attacked him so fiercely that the poor fellow was nearly torn to pieces. His limbs and torn flesh were tossed aside contemptuously. His descendants still hide among the rocks and in salt water pools as their ancestor did that day, and their bodies bear the marks of the fury of Whale when he turned against his friend. But little Starfish had not submitted to punishment without some resistance, and in his struggles he managed to tear a hole in Whale's head, which is also inherited by the descendants of their huge ancestor.

Whale raced across the ocean with water vapour roaring from the hole in his head, and began to overtake the canoe. The terrified animals dug their paddles deeper in the water and strained every muscle to make the canoe go faster, but it was mainly through the efforts of Koala that they managed to keep at a safe distance from their infuriated pursuer.

'Look at my strong arms,' cried Native Bear. 'Take your paddle strokes from me.' The gap grew wider as his powerful arms made the paddle fly through the water, and ever since his arms have been strong and muscular.

The chase continued for several days and nights, until at last land came in sight—the country they had longed for. At the entrance to Lake Illawarra the canoe was grounded and the animals jumped ashore. As they disappeared into the bush the canoe rose and fell on the waves. Brolga, the Native Companion, was the only one who had the presence of mind to remember that they would never be safe while Whale was free to roam the seas in his canoe, for at any time he might come ashore and take up the pursuit again. So Brolga pushed the canoe out from the shore and danced and stamped on the thin bark until it was broken and sank beneath the waves. There it turned to stone; and it can still be seen as the island of Canman-gang near the entrance to Lake Illawarra. Ever since that day Brolga has continued the dance that broke up the canoe.

Whale turned aside in disgust and swam away up the coast, as his descendants still do. As for the animal-men, they explored the land and found it as good as the birds had said. They settled there, making their homes in trees and caves, by rivers and lakes, in the bush, and on the endless plains of the interior.

 ## How Flying Fox Divided Day and Night

In the first corroboree at the beginning of time, birds and animals mixed happily together and joined in the dances. The tribes vied with each other. Cockatoo, who was vain, sidled up to Eagle-hawk, the leader of the birds, and said, 'There is no doubt that birds are better performers than animals, is there?'

'No doubt at all,' said Eagle-hawk.

Cockatoo bustled off and told all his friends that Eagle-hawk had said that birds were better than animals. Before long Kangaroo, who was the natural leader of the animal tribes, was told what the birds were saying. He went to Eagle-hawk to remonstrate with him, but the bird-man was so stubborn that the two began to quarrel. Tempers rose, others joined in the argument, and in a short space of time blows were struck, and a battle began. The animal-men fought against the bird-men; the only ones who were uncertain about the dispute were Flying Fox and Owl. They conferred together.

'The sensible thing to do is to join the winning side,' Owl advised his friend.

'But how do we know who will win?'

'We will not move hastily. Let us wait for a while in the shade of this tree. We can rest, and when we are sure how the battle is going, we will know what to do.'

They reclined in comfort, watching the birds and animals swaying backwards and forwards as their fortunes ebbed and flowed. Weapons flashed and were dulled with blood. Gradually the animals were forced backwards. Cheered by their success, the birds redoubled their efforts.

'Come on,' shouted Owl. 'We are bird-men. To the defence of our brothers!'

They made themselves conspicuous, and with their support the birds seemed to be overcoming their opponents.

But in the rear of the animals Kangaroo was mustering a fresh band of highly-trained warriors. They stole behind the trees and burst unexpectedly into the ranks of the birds, who reeled under the shock. The animals who had been so hard-pressed rallied their forces, and in a short time the position was reversed. The birds had to defend themselves against the animals who were bitterly avenging the deaths of their friends.

'You made a mistake,' Flying Fox hissed.

'Don't worry,' Owl replied. 'Everyone makes mistakes. It is a wise person who realises it.'

He turned round and belaboured the birds with his nullanulla, and Flying Fox reluctantly followed his example. As the tide of battle raged to and fro, Kangaroo and Eagle-hawk found themselves facing each other. They were so weary that they could hardly raise their clubs. Eagle-hawk dropped his to the ground.

'What are we really fighting about, Kangaroo?' he asked. 'If I offended you by my boasting I am sorry for it.'

'You were boastful,' Kangaroo said thoughtfully, 'but perhaps you had good cause. Certainly it is not worth fighting about. Let us be friends as we were before.'

They called to their followers to cease fighting. Once again Flying Fox and Owl found themselves in an awkward position. They had fought for the birds, and then for the animals, and now they knew that no one would trust them. They went off and hid in the bush. The light paled, and presently the darkness became impenetrable.

'This is good,' Owl remarked. 'We can both see in the dark; but the other birds and animals need light. They'll never find us now.'

But they were puzzled that it should be so dark when it was many hours till sunset. They did not know that Yhi had been so grieved at the fighting that she had hidden her light from her creatures. The darkness that had brought relief to Owl and Flying Fox had brought distress to others. They could not see to gather food, nor even to find their homes, or their dead relatives. They stumbled over stones and blundered into trees, while there seemed to be no end to the all-pervading blackness.

Two dim shapes met with a shock.

'Who are you?' asked one of them. 'I am Emu.'

'I am Kangaroo.'

'Kangaroo, you are wise,' Emu said. 'Tell us what we must do to save ourselves.'

'I have been thinking about it. We must light fires—many fires. By their light we shall be able to find food and cook it, and we can warm ourselves, and know that we are men again.'

Birds and animals scurried about picking up dead wood, and soon the cheerful glow of firelight flickered on the sandy ground among the bushes. It was a strange, shadowy world: outside the circles of light the gloom seemed more intense than before. The animals dragged big logs to their encampment, and the smaller birds were kept busy fossicking for chips and dry twigs, but it was not long before the supply of wood was exhausted.

Kangaroo called everyone together to discuss the matter. No one had any solution to the problem until one of the smaller lizards said, 'Why don't we ask Owl and Flying Fox to tell us what to do? They might have the answer to our problem.'

'It would do no harm to ask them, but where are they?' Kangaroo asked. 'Ever since they proved themselves traitors they have been hiding, and we could never find them now in the darkness outside the firelight.'

'I think I know where they have gone,' little Lizard said. 'I'll try to find them if you like.'

'Very well,' Kangaroo said with a smile. 'Off you go.'

Lizard scuttled off into the darkness.

'Where are you, Owl? Where are you, Flying Fox?' he kept calling. Presently there was an answering cry, and he saw Owl sitting up on the branch of a tree.

'What do you want, little Lizard?'

'We want you and Flying Fox to come to our meeting and tell us how to get the light back again. Listen!'

In the stillness they heard a dismal wailing.

'That is Dingo and Curlew. They go on like that all the time. They are waiting for the sunlight.'

'Oh, no,' Owl said. 'If we went with you we would be killed. Don't you know that we have offended everybody?'

'No one will touch you,' Lizard said earnestly. 'We are too sad and frightened. All we want is someone to tell us how to get rid of the darkness.'

'Very well then, we will take the risk.' Owl raised his voice. 'Come, Flying Fox,' he called.

Together the three men, bird, animal, and lizard, went back to the main camp, which could be identified only by the dull glow of the dying embers.

'Is it you, Owl and Flying Fox?' asked Kangaroo.

'Yes. We have come to see what you want.'

'Do you know how to dispel the darkness?'

'Yes.'

'Will you help us, then?'

Owl gave an evil chuckle.

'Why should we help you? We have no love for you, and you only want us for what we can give you. Darkness is a good thing—good for hunting, good for living in. You had better get used to it.'

'But ...' began Flying Fox.

'Don't be silly,' Owl said quickly. 'You know very well that the birds and animals wouldn't do anything for us. Let us go at once.'

Kangaroo and Emu tried to catch them, but like two shadows, they vanished into the darkness. Behind them rose a sad cry, 'O Uncle, give us back the light. O Uncle ...' The voices died away; but as despair settled on the gathering, Flying Fox suddenly appeared among them again.

'I cannot leave you like this,' he said. 'I have been influenced by Owl far too much. I am half bird and half animal, so I am kin to everyone. I will help you. Can someone lend me a boomerang?'

'Here you are,' half a dozen voices said eagerly.

Flying Fox chose one that the little Lizard held out to him, balanced it carefully, and threw it towards the north. It flew up and over the earth like a streak of light, turned in a wide circle, and came back over their heads from the south. Flying Fox caught it deftly and threw it to the east. When it returned from the west, Flying Fox prepared to throw it for the third time. Emu could tolerate this game no longer. He caught Flying Fox by the shoulder.

'We asked you to bring back the light, Flying Fox,' he said roughly. 'Why do you keep throwing the returning boomerang? Anyone could do that.'

Flying Fox shook himself free.

'I am doing what I promised. I am cutting the darkness in two. I will give the light to you, but I will keep the darkness for myself.'

He threw the boomerang to the west. They watched it speeding like a meteor, curving gently at the end of its flight, circling towards the north, then to the south, and finally to the east. As it came towards them it brought the light with it—light which flooded the plain and shone on their anxious faces.

'There you are,' said Flying Fox. 'Remember that the darkness came because your hearts were evil, not mine. It was you who fought against each other. It was Lizard who braved the terrors of the night to find me, and it was he who gave me the boomerang. For that he will always carry the sign of the boomerang on his neck. I will take my share now and leave you to enjoy the warm sunshine,' and with these words he left them, taking the darkness with him, and hid it in the cave where he had made his home.

The selfishness of Owl has never been forgotten by the birds who have descended from the bird-men. At night he is safe but if he ventures out in the early dusk, he is mobbed by the other birds. But if Flying Fox flies out of his cave while it is still light, he knows that he will be safe. No one will molest him because of the memory of how he brought the sun to the world when men had despaired of ever seeing it again.

 ## The Imprisonment of Narahdarn the Bat

Narahdarn the Bat was a man who enjoyed darkness, and the evil that is performed in darkness. He had married Wahlillee and Goonaroo, the daughters of Bilbie the Rabbit-eared Bandicoot. They were industrious young women who employed all their time in gathering food. Narahdarn lived a life of luxury, seldom going out on the hunting trail, but growing fat and indolent on the food that his women brought to him.

For a long time they pandered to their husband, but at last they grew tired of working so hard and decided that it was better to have no husband than one who lived off his wives. They made long strings of dried reeds and clothed themselves in them so they rattled with every movement they made.

Wahlillie and Goonaroo waited until Narahdarn was away visiting friends in another tribe, and hid themselves beside the path they knew he must follow on his return.

After a while Narahdarn and his dog came unsuspectingly along this path. The women jumped out with blood-curdling screams, with the reeds flying round them in a cloud and clashing together. Narahdarn reeled back, turned, and fled with his dog. He could not see very well in the daylight, and bruised himself by banging into tree trunks. He dared not turn round, for he was frightened of the apparitions, and he was fast growing weak and tired. Suddenly he crashed into a tree, saw that it was hollow, and squeezed himself through the opening, followed by his dog.

The women looked at each other, and the same thought occurred to them simultaneously. They scooped mud from the ground and plastered it over the opening. Then they stood on guard till it dried, and Narahdarn and the dog were safely imprisoned in the tree. The man heard their laughter dying away in the distance, and began to scrape the mud with his fingernails, but it had become as hard as the timber of the tree in which he was imprisoned.

Shut up in the dark with little room to move, the hours and days seemed like an eternity. His biggest problem was hunger and thirst. The only food that could sustain him was the flesh of his dog, but Narahdarn could not bear the thought of eating his only friend. Instead, he told the dog to tear the flesh of his arm, and when it had done so, the man drank his own blood to quench his thirst.

Many days passed by. The dog died and lay still at his feet. Then Narahdarn heard the sound of wood being chopped nearby. He shouted, and the sound echoed in the narrow confines of his prison. The sound of axe blows stopped. The woodcutter felt the hairs on his scalp rising as words came indistinctly from the tree.

'Who are you?' he asked, his voice trembling.

'I am a man. I am imprisoned in this tree. My name is Narahdarn.'

'What are you doing in there?'

'I was caught when I sought shelter. Please help me.'

'How can I help you?'

'Look at the dried mud on the trunk, friend. I have no tool to scrape it away, but you could break it down with your axe.'

'How do I know that you are not an evil spirit that will do me harm if I release you?'

'Spirits cannot be shut up in trees. I am a man, weak and at the point of death, for I have been here many days.'

The woodcutter was convinced that it was the tone of a man who was close to death. He summoned up his courage, and soon the mud filling crumbled under the blows of his axe. Then he leapt back in alarm. It was scarcely the figure of a man who came out of the narrow prison. It was a skeleton that lived and moved. From its arms hung rags and tatters of skin that flapped as he walked. The woodcutter dropped his tool and raced for home to tell a tale that no one would believe.

Once he was free Narahdarn's heart was black and heavy with vengeance. He rested for a few days to recover his strength, and to allow his wounds to heal. His body began to fill out, but his mind was an empty dish in which ugly thoughts rolled and clashed unceasingly.

With the axe that the woodcutter had left behind in his haste, he cut two long stakes and pointed them at both ends. Taking them down to the river, he drove them deep into the bed below the bank at the place where his wives usually fished, and returned to his own camp. Wahlillee and Goonaroo were making preparations for the evening meal when their husband appeared suddenly in front of them.

He grunted as though nothing unusual had happened, and said, 'I am hungry. Go and catch some fish for me.'

The young women rushed off in a panic.

'What shall we do?' Goonaroo asked her sister. 'He will kill us!'

'I don't know,' Wahlillee replied, 'but first of all let us catch some fish. That may put him in a good mood, and we can make plans when he falls asleep.'

They jumped into the water with their nets, and were immediately impaled on the hidden stakes.

Presently Narahdarn came sauntering along the bank. He pulled Wahlillee out of the water and threw her body on the ground. With rather more interest he watched Goonaroo, who was still struggling feebly in the water, trying to release herself from the stake which had gone through her throat.

Her husband sat down to watch, nodding approvingly when she managed to release herself and struggle to the bank. The breath whistled through the hole in her throat. Her fat body grew still plumper, her legs and feet shrank, her arms turned into wings. In despair she tried to call out to Narahdarn, but her voice whistled in her throat and sounded as though she was saying 'Goonaroo! Goonaroo!' She flapped her wings and flew across the water, disappearing into the twilight. And still we may hear the call of the Whistling Duck as she calls her own name—Goonaroo, Goonaroo.

Narahdarn remained alone in the deserted camp. The death of his wives was not the sweet revenge he had anticipated. Now he had to hunt for meat and vegetables, and cook his own food. No laughter now by the camp fire at night; no comfort in the warm body of a woman by his side; not even the friendship of his dog.

One day he was visited by Bilbie the younger, the brother of his wives. Bilbie looked round the untidy camp with distaste.

'Where are my sisters?'

'I don't know. They went away and left me.'

'It was your laziness that drove them away,' Bilbie said. He left the camp and called the people of his tribe together.

'Narahdarn is living alone,' he told them. 'Wahlillie and Goonaroo are not with him now. If they had left him of their own accord they would have come back to us.'

'What do you mean, Bilbie?' someone asked. 'If Narahdarn says they left him, where could they have gone?'

There was a little silence. Far away they heard the voice of Goonaroo the Whistling Duck.

'They are dead,' Bilbie said suddenly. 'I know it. Narahdarn has killed them.'

There was a chorus of grunts. A young man stood up and waved his spear.

'What are we waiting for? Our sisters have been killed and we sit round the fire like old men brooding over their troubles.'

Others jumped up to join him. Darkness had fallen when the men reached Narahdarn's encampment. He was sitting by the fire when a spear thudded into the ground at his feet. He whirled round and saw his wives' kinsmen coming stealthily towards him. He sprang from side to side, trying to escape the spears that hurtled from every direction. In a frenzy of fear he leaped higher and higher, and the torn skin of his arms flapped against his body.

Bilbie aimed a murderous blow at him. Narahdarn jumped even higher in the air, his arms waving. As his body dwindled and his head and legs grew small, he remembered what he had done to Goonaroo. Like a dark, evil shadow, he fled to the shelter of the trees. He was no longer a man flying through the dark, but Narahdarn the Bat. His refuge was the hollow tree where the spirit of his dog awaited him, and in hollow trees he has remained through all the years.

He is Narahdarn, the Bat, the spirit of death, who flies by night and sleeps by day.

 ## Why Platypus Lives Alone

When the first men became animals, the country was so thickly populated by birds, lizards, and snakes, that it became impossible for them to live together in peace. There was not enough food, so the weaker ones died of starvation if they did not meet a sudden death. While birds preyed on reptiles, reptiles on animals, and animals on birds, not one of them was safe. To drop off to sleep was to run the danger of never waking again, or to feel the bite of sharp teeth, the spearlike thrust of a beak, or the poison fang of a snake before life ebbed quickly away.

At length, remembering the corroborees that they had held while they were still men, they all met together to discuss what should be done. The snakes spoke first.

'We are tired of being hunted by birds and animals. Only this morning several of our people were eaten by the kookaburras. Snakes have as much right to live as anyone else. We are an inoffensive tribe.'

'But you rob our nests,' the birds accused them. 'If the eggs escape you, you take our fledglings. Our nests should be left alone.'

There was an outcry from the animals.

'Do you respect our children? It is when they are young and defenceless that you kill them without thought of the sorrow you are bringing to us.'

'Enough!' shouted the leader of the snakes. 'We all have the right to live, snakes as well as anyone else. We have debated the matter in our own tribe. There is only one solution to the problem.'

'What is it? What is it?'

'You must go away and leave us in peace. The land belongs to us reptiles. There is no place here for birds and animals.'

A chorus of derisive laughter rose, led by Kookaburra.

'If anyone leaves, it will be you reptiles.'

'No, it will be you. We are a humble people. We creep along the ground and try to make ourselves inconspicuous, but we have a weapon that is denied to you. Long years ago the Crow gave us poison fangs. We would not like to keep on using them on you.'

Such a babble of voices now arose that no one could be heard, and the meeting broke up in disorder.

Of all the reptiles, the frilled lizards were the most vicious. Their leaders called them together to discuss what had happened at the corroboree.

'The snakes made threats, but they talk too much. The animals and birds need a real fright. The snakes are only making them fighting mad. We have no poison fangs, but we must remember our totem. There is no need to tell you what to do.'

The totem of the frilled lizards was the wild elements of nature: thunder and lightning, wind and rain and storm. Leaving the other people of the lizard tribe behind, they swarmed up the nearest mountain until they reached the summit where they were close to the spirits of the storm. They painted their bodies with a mixture of fat and red ochre, and lined them with bands of white clay; they were a fearsome sight. Then they gashed themselves with stone knives until the blood ran down their bodies and mingled with the painted designs, and they sang the song that conjures up the storm.

So many frilled lizards sang that weird song that black clouds raced across the sky and pressed heavily on the mountain top. Lightning flashed in the gloom and thunder rolled down the long valleys. Then came the rain … driving spears and splinters of silver that slashed into the trees and dug pits in the dry ground. The pits filled with water, overflowed into runnels that grew to streams, and streams into rivers that spilled into lakes. The lakes rose until the tops of tall trees were lost beneath the surging water.

The birds fled from the storm, while the reptiles and animals crouched in caves, shivered under the poor shelter of trees, or climbed the mountainside to escape the advancing water. With a final peal of thunder the storm rolled away. For many days and nights the storm spirits had hurled their weapons against the defenceless earth. Blue skies returned and the sun shone until the land steamed, and bedraggled animals stretched out to feel the unaccustomed warmth.

They searched for their friends among the fallen trees. Everywhere they went they found pathetic bodies of platypuses, who were so slow-moving that they had been unable to escape from the flood waters. Before the storm they had been the most numerous of all animals. Now not a single one could be found.

Several years passed by. The birds returned, and as children were born to the animals, the strength of the tribes increased; but there were still no platypuses. Even those who had been impatient with them in the past regretted their loss. Others sorrowed, and sought everywhere to see if there were any survivors. Hope revived when far-ranging Cormorant came one day with a report that he had seen playtpus tracks in the mud at a place somewhere between the Blue Mountains and the sea. A carpet snake, returning from a visit to distant relatives, also related that as he was watching a pool he had seen a hole under water which led into the bank, and which he recognised as the entrance to the burrow of a platypus.

There was great excitement at the news. Animals of all kinds met together to talk about it. The only absentees were the frilled lizards. Everyone knew that they had been responsible for the flood which had destroyed the poor little platypuses. They had been told that they would not be welcome at the gathering. The lizards puffed out their frills in vexation and wore frowning faces, which they have never since managed to get rid of.

'What totem do the platypuses belong to?' someone asked.

Everybody seemed to join the discussion. Because they had ducks' heads and laid eggs, the birds claimed that platypuses were really birds; but the lizards and snakes had an equal claim because they too were egg-layers. Kangaroos, possums, wallabies, and many other animals maintained that as platypuses had bodies covered with hair, as well as tails, they undoubtedly belonged to the animal family. No one could resolve these contradictory statements, especially when the fish joined in and pointed out that platypuses spent a good deal of their time under water.

'We need to hear what they have to say for themselves,' one of the leaders said. 'If someone will volunteer to go beyond the mountains, it may be that they will find the platypus family that Cormorant and Carpet Snake have reported.'

It was agreed that this was a good plan. As Carpet Snake knew where the place was, he agreed to make the journey. To everyone's satisfaction he returned a few days later with an old and venerable platypus, who was at once surrounded by an eager throng of animals, birds, and reptiles, anxious to do all they could to show how glad they were to see him.

When the excitement died down, a space was cleared, and the old platypus began to speak. At first his voice was low and unsteady, because he was not used to company, but gradually it grew stronger and he could be heard by all his listeners.

'My friends, you have asked me to tell you what people we belong to. Ever since the great flood we have been isolated. We have felt that no one wanted us; but as you assure me that you are all my friends, we shall be glad to come back.

'We come from an ancient race, renowned for their wisdom, and we claim kinship with you all. Our first ancestors were reptiles. Later we belonged to the family of birds. Lastly we became animals.'

The platypus was interrupted by a buzz of conversation; he raised his paws and silence fell once more.

'Where is Theen-who-ween?'

They looked at each other in bewilderment until Emu strode to the front.

'Why is *he* coming forward?' they whispered to each other. 'His name is Pinyali.'

Emu addressed Platypus.

'You have called me by the name that was given to my fathers, but is known to no one of this present generation except myself. Great is your wisdom and knowledge, Platypus.'

Emu embraced him and said, 'Tell me, O wise one, what is your totem?'

'The totem of the Platypus is the Bandicoot. What is your totem?'

'Our totem is the Snake.'

'Then, as I have already told you, we are all kin.'

'No, no,' Emu said hastily. 'We would welcome you into our family of birds. Your young men should marry Emu girls.'

Platypus looked at him sadly.

'You tell me that the totem of a bird is the Snake, and I say that our totem is an animal. I will consult my uncle Bandicoot.'

'But Bandicoot is my uncle,' Emu said, more puzzled than before.

'It is as I say. The platypus is akin to you all, yet he cannot marry you. We are alone. It has been planned from the beginning of time, and we must accept the decision of Baiame the Great Spirit.'

He made his way through the crowd, which parted in front of him, and walked slowly and sadly back to his home. When he got there he found the friendly bandicoots waiting for him.

'We shall never leave you,' they told him. 'We are your people, and you are ours. Show us your sons.'

Then the bandicoot girls married the young platypus boys when they reached manhood and passed the initiation ceremonies. Everyone left them alone, except the water rats, who were jealous of the bandicoots. The water rats attacked the combined tribes, but were driven back by spears and other weapons, and many of them were killed.

So Platypus, who is of no tribe, yet of every tribe, lives alone, on land and in the water; and thanks the ancient gods who made him as he is.

 How Kangaroo Got his Tail

Mirram the Kangaroo and Warreen the Wombat, walking on two legs as men, were friends. They lived together, but each had his own way of doing things. Warreen built a gunyah, a little house made of bark, to protect himself from the rain, a place where he could light a fire and sleep in comfort on cold nights. Mirram was much more of an outdoor man. He loved to lie out in the open at night where he could see the stars shining through the leaves of the trees and feel the wind on his face. Sometimes he persuaded Warreen to leave his gunyah and spend the night with him, but Wombat never felt really happy unless he was curled up inside his hut.

During the summer the friends lived happily together, but it was different in the winter. One night a bitter wind blew across the land. Mirram huddled up against the trunk of a tree and tried to keep warm by rolling himself into a ball; he was still proud of the way he could face the weather while his timid companion hid under the bark roof of a stuffy hut. He laughed a little at the thought of Warreen crouched in the tiny gunyah.

After a while it begun to rain. Not a light shower, but sheets of icy water that were driven by the wind, soaking him from head to foot. It was no use trying to shelter under the trees. The branches were lashing like snakes in the wind, adding to the raindrops that were hurled under them by the wind. The thought of Warreen's cosy little gunyah suddenly became very attractive.

He imagined what it would be like inside, with the bark walls lit by the flames of the fire, and the lovely feeling he would have as he stretched out in front of it, warm and dry. He could bear the thought no longer. Fighting his way against wind and rain, he came to the gunyah and knocked against the wall.

'Who is it?' asked a sleepy voice.

'It's me, Mirram. I'm wet and cold. May I come in?'

Warreen laughed. 'Oh no, it can't be you, Mirram. You like sleeping out in the fresh air. It must be someone trying to imitate your voice. I'm scared.'

'Open the door,' Kangaroo called sharply. 'This is no time for playing. I'm frozen.'

'But you like it that way,' Warreen replied. 'Remember, I offered to help you build a gunyah for yourself, but you said it was silly to hide from the wind and the rain. Besides, there's no room in here.'

Mirram forced his way through the narrow doorway.

'I'm here,' he said. 'What are you going to do about it?'

'If you must come in, put the door back after you. Stand over there in the corner. You're wet, and you're waking me up.'

Mirram sniffed.

'Move over,' he said, his teeth chattering with the cold. 'I must get dry before I can talk.'

'But I don't want to talk. I want to go to sleep again. If you stand against the wall you'll soon get dry, but don't come near me.'

He stretched himself out in front of the fire and went back to sleep. Mirram was crowded into a corner where there was a crack in the bark. The rain poured through it, and whenever he moved the draught seemed to follow him. When his front was dry he turned round to let the fire warm his back. Warreen snored gently, and the fire died down until there was only a dull red glow from the embers.

Bitter thoughts circled round inside Mirram's head. He beat his arms against his body to keep warm. When morning came he hobbled outside, picked up a large stone which was half buried in the mud, and staggered back to the hut. Warreen was stretching himself lazily and looking round to see where Mirram had gone. Kangaroo stepped inside, raised the stone at arm's length, and smashed it against Warreen's head, flattening the front part of his skull.

'There!' he said, 'that will teach you to neglect a friend. You'll always have a flat forehead now to remind you of your unkindness. I'll tell you another thing too, friend Wombat. From now on you'll always live in this dark, damp hole you call your home.'

From that day Kangaroo and Wombat never spoke to each other. Warreen planned revenge. He cut a big spear and made a woomera to help him throw the spear much better than he could manage with his tiny paws.

He had a long time to wait, but at last his opportunity came. Mirram's back was turned and the woomera was in the right position. He threw it with all his might. The spear whistled through the air and struck Mirram at the base of his spine.

'There!' shouted Warreen, as Mirram let out a yell of pain and fright. 'That'll teach you to knock me about!'

Kangaroo tugged at the spear, but he could not move it. Wombat laughed and laughed until he rolled right back into his burrow.

'You've got a tail now,' he said as he disappeared from sight. 'Mirram has got a tail, and no home to go to. Serves him right!'

 The Cat Killer

Kinie-ger was on the hunting trail, and terror stalked through the land. Kinie-ger had the body and limbs of a man and the head of a cat. He was a voracious eater. No one would have held that against him, for both men and animals must live on flesh as well as vegetable food; but Kinie-ger was an insensate killer, destroying living things for the pleasure of seeing them die. No one was safe from him. Tiny children, young people and old folk, all were afraid when Kinie-ger was abroad.

The men did their best to protect the weaker members of their tribe, standing on guard throughout the night, but they were unable to maintain a watch throughout the day, for there were many other things to be done. If everyone had stayed within the limits of the encampment all would have been well, but the younger folk would not submit to too much restraint. Apart from this it was necessary for young and old alike to spend time hunting for food, which could not always be obtained close to the camp. Many lovely girls never returned to their parents. Their mangled bodies were found only when a search was made for them.

The men of the Kangaroo tribe took counsel together and determined to hunt Kinie-ger down and put him to death so that the shadow of fear might be lifted from their people. Going out in small parties, armed with spear, boomerang, and nullanulla, they spread out over the plain, beating the bushes, but all in vain. The wily Cat-man had seen them coming and hid himself where no one could find him.

Another Kangaroo council was held. The wisest men said that only by combining with other tribes could they hope to put an end to Kinie-ger. It took many days to gather all the tribesmen together, but at length a great encampment was formed. Many armed men went out, determined not to return until they brought with them the lifeless body of Kinie-ger.

Three days later the last of them straggled back, dejected and ashamed, for of Kinie-ger they had found not the slightest sign.

'Perhaps he is not an animal at all,' someone suggested. 'Maybe he is a spirit sent to punish us.'

There were some who thought that this might be true, but others said, 'The work that has been done on the bodies of our women and children is truly the work of an animal. No spirit would flay the skin from their bodies and eat the flesh.'

'We are powerless against Kinie-ger,' an old man said. 'He can do as he wills with us. When we seek him he can vanish like a spirit, even though he is an animal-man. There is only one way to find him.'

'What is that?' several men shouted.

'If we can find him, we can kill him,' the other man went on.

There were cries of annoyance. 'Tell us what thoughts are in your head, old man, or it will be you that is killed.'

The old man took his time. He looked up at the sky, scratched himself reflectively, and at last said, 'We cannot do it by ourselves. Let us ask Eagle-hawk and Owl.'

He held up his hand.

'Listen. There is wisdom in my thoughts. Eagle-hawk can see from afar. Nothing can hide from him except by night. In the dark Owl will stare with his big eyes, and we shall find Kinie-ger. If we can find him we can kill him,' he said again triumphantly.

The advice was talked over and found good. Eagle-hawk and Owl promised to help, and plans were made. There was to be no premature move.

The Kangaroo tribe waited through the dry weather until the ground was parched and leaves hung limply from the trees. Everyone was consumed by thirst. On a hot morning under a cloudless sky, when the whole land was covered with a haze of dust and smoke from distant fires, the men went to every water hole but one.

'The time has come,' the old man said.

He led Eagle-hawk and Owl to the last water hole, and the three of them dug a pit, into which Owl and Eagle-hawk jumped so that they were hidden from sight, while the old man returned to the camp.

The land lay silent, quivering in the heat which rose in shimmering waves above the earth. Owl and Eagle-hawk were silent too, listening for the sound of footsteps. In the late afternoon they heard a soft pad, pad, padding, and then the sound of someone lapping water. Eagle-hawk peered cautiously from his hiding place. Slowly the two birds' heads rose above the ground, and two pairs of eyes stared intently at the water hole.

Kinie-ger was lying flat on his stomach, his weapons by his side, lapping thirstily at the unguarded water. Owl and Eagle-hawk climbed stealthily and silently out of the pit, tiptoed to the water hole, and plunged their spears into the back of Kinie-ger.

The stars had appeared by the time the bird men brought the news of the killing of Kinie-ger to the Kangaroo tribe. Through the darkness a laughing, chattering, shouting crowd of men, women, and children ran to see the body of the hated Cat-man. Before they reached it they saw a star rising from the water hole, moving steadily up into the sky, where it remained shining brightly.

Kinie-ger was no longer by the edge of the water hole. All they could find was the body of a small grey animal covered with white spots. Every head was turned towards the old man who had planned the death of the Cat-man. He grinned fiercely and shook his waddy.

'This is Kinie-ger,' he said. 'The courage of Owl and Eagle-hawk has brought about his death, but I have rid you of his spirit, which will never come down from the sky. There it is,' pointing dramatically up at the new star, 'and here is all that remains of the Cat-man—this little animal.'

'How do we know that this is really Kinie-ger?' someone asked.

The old man bent down and showed them the white spots in the grey fur.

'Those are the wounds that Owl and Eagle-hawk made with their spears. Every time you see the little Kinie-ger, the cat that has taken the place of the Cat-man, you must remember the spear thrusts that killed him. You must remember Owl and Eagle-hawk in gratitude, because you need no longer fear the death that pounces from the bush when you are alone. And you must remember that it was my magic that set you free of fear.'

Glossary

Bahloo: the moon god
Baiame: the Great Spirit
Baiamul: black swan
Bibbi: woodpecker
Bilbie: rabbit-eared bandicoot
billabong: isolated river pool
Birra-nulu: wife of Baiame
boomerang: throwing weapon
Booran: pelican
bora: initiation ceremony
Brolga: native companion
Bullima: spirit world
Bu-maya-mul: wood lizard
bunyip: monster of the swamp
Bunyun-bunyun: frog
Butterga: flying squirrel
Cheeroonear: dog-faced man
churinga: bullroarer (and other sacred objects)
coolabah: tree
coolamon: wooden drinking vessel
Deegeenboya: soldier bird
Deereeree: willy wagtail
dilly: string bag for carrying possessions
Dinewan: emu
Du-mer: brown pigeon
Eer-moonan: monsters
Ga-ra-gah: blue crane
Gidgeereegah: budgerigar or warbling grass parrot
Googoorewon: the place of trees
Goomblegubbon: bustard or brush turkey

Goonaroo: whistling duck, wife of Narahdarn and daughter of Bilbie
Goorgourgahgah: kookaburra
gunyah: hut
Gurangatch: water monster
humpy: hut
In-nard-dooah: porcupine
Keen Keengs: flying men descended from giants
Kinie-ger: native cat
Kubbitha: black duck, wife of Mungoongarlie
Kunnan-beili: wife of Baiame
kurria: crocodile guardian
Madhi: dog
Maira: paddy-melon
maldape: monster
mallee: eucalypt scrub
Marmoo: spirit of evil
Mar-rallang: wives of Wyungare
Meamei: the Pleiades, the Seven Sisters
miamia: hut
Millin-nulu-nubba: small bird
mingga: a spirit
Mirragen: cat
Mirram: kangaroo
Moodai: possum
Moograbah: bell magpie
Mullian: eagle-hawk
Mullian-ga: morning star, leader of the Mullians
Mungoongarlie: giant goanna
Murga-muggai: trapdoor spider
Murra-wunda: climbing rat
Narahdarn: bat
Nepelle: ruler of the heavens

Noyang: eel

nullanulla: club

Nungeena: mother spirit

Nurunderi: servant of Nepelle

Ooboon: blue-tongued lizard

Ouyarh: cockatoo

Ouyouboolooey: black snake

Pinyali: emu

Puckowie: the grandmother spirit

Punjel: spirit who rules in Milky Way with Baiame

Theen-who-ween: ancient name for emu

Tuckonies: tree spirits, or spirits of growth

tukkeri: fish forbidden to women

Tya: the earth

Wahlillie: wife of Narahdarn and daughter of Bilbie

Wahn: crow

Walla-gudjail-uan: spirit of birth

Walla-guroon-buan: a spirit

Warreen: wombat

Wayambeh: tortoise

Whowhie: monster of the Murray River

willywilly: whirlwind

wirinun: medicine man or priest

wirrie: stick to extract poison from dead body

Woggoon: mallee fowl

woomera: throwing stick

Wunda: evil spirit

Wungghee: mopoke

wurley: hut

Wurrawilberoo: whirlwind or whirlwind devil

Wyungare: 'he who returns to the stars'

yacca: grass tree

yaraan: a tree
Yara-ma-yha-who: a monster
Yarrageh: spirit of spring
Yee-na-pah: mountain devil
Yhi: sun goddess

Other Books in This Series By A. W. Reed

Aboriginal Words of Australia   Words used by Aboriginal tribes and their meanings. Contains a useful English-Aboriginal section.

Aboriginal Place Names   A comprehensive collection of names and their derivations from all parts of Australia. Includes a section giving English words and their Aboriginal translations, as well as an appendix of present day names with their earlier Aboriginal names.

Aboriginal Fables   A varied collection of Aboriginal folk tales and legends about animal life and nature and the creation of the world.

Aboriginal Legends   A large selection of Aboriginal legends dealing mainly with the origin of different forms of animal life. The legends come from a variety of tribes from all parts of the continent.

Aboriginal Myths   Myths of the first creation by the Great Spirit, myths of totemic ancestors and myths dealing with the origin of natural phenomena and specific features of animal life.

Aboriginal Tales of Australia   This companion volume to *Aboriginal Stories of Australia* presents a further twenty-two stories that are a rich reflection of Aboriginal thought and culture.